DIANA S. ZIMMERMAN

KANDIDE
and the
SECRET of the MISTS™

THE CALABIYAU CHRONICLES Book One
ILLUSTRATIONS BY MAXINE GADD

Noesis Publishing™
Los Angeles

Text copyright ©2008 by Diana S. Zimmerman
Illustrations copyright ©2008 by Maxine Gadd

Noesis logo trademark Noesis Publishing
Kandide and the Secret of the Mists logo trademark Diana S. Zimmerman
All rights reserved under all copyright conventions.

First Edition, Revised

ISBN: 978-0-9794328-2-8
Library of Congress Control Number: 2007942101
Zimmerman, Diana S.
Kandide and the Secret of the Mists/Diana S. Zimmerman;
Illustrations by Maxine Gadd. — 1st Ed.

1. Princesses—Juvenile fiction. 2. Perfection—Juvenile fiction. 3. Fairies—
Juvenile fiction. 4. Calabiyau (Imaginary place)—Juvenile fiction. 5. Princesses—
Fiction. 6. Perfection—Fiction. 7. Fairies—Fiction. 8. Fantasy
fiction. I. Gadd, Maxine, 1962— II. Title.

PZ7.Z56 Ka 2008
[Fic]   2007942101

11 10 09 08 10 9 8 7 6 5 4 3 2 1

Published by Noesis Publishing
A division of Noesis Communications International, Inc.
5777 W. Century Blvd., #200
Los Angeles, CA 90045
(310) 645-5604
www.noesispublishing.com

Cover Design by Stephanie Lostimolo
Book Design by Imaginosis Media Design/Greenleaf Book Group LP

For ordering information or special discounts for bulk purchases, please contact Greenleaf Book Group LP at: 4425 South Mo Pac Expwy., Suite 600 Austin, TX 78735, (512) 891-6100.

Kandide and the Secret of the Mists is dedicated to:

Cynthia Unninayar, who inspired my faery collection; Alice Shultz, who read the first faery story to me; and Stan Shultz, who believed.

As well as those who read, reread, criticized, improved, proofed, and reproofed every page: Dawn Abel, Candice Adams, Sal and Marie Barilla, Tracy Charles, Jeanie Cunningham, Jonathon Debach, Bob Dorian, Paul Elliott, Patricia Fry, Robert Gould, Patrick Grady, Karen Grim, Carol Ivy, Bruce Merrin, Lee and Dan Merrin, Cameron King, Dennis Mullican, Caryn Parker, Brian Sharp, and S. Earl Statler.

With special thanks to my twenty-one junior editors from Sabal Point Elementary School: Alexis, Amanda, Annika, Brianna, Bryanna, Cameron, Christian, Christina, Dakota, Elliot, Ignacio, Jassem, Jacob, J. J., Justin, Kinely, Samantha, Shannon, Taylor, Victoria, Zachary, and their extraordinary teacher, Jeff Smith.

THE LANDS OF CALABIYAU

Known to scholars as the elemental dimension, Calabiyau is the realm of the Fée. It is a world that exists in parallel time and space with our own. Spreading across the region we refer to as middle Europe, this enigmatic land has long been overlooked by all but the most perceptive of humans. Time passes far more slowly, magic is as normal as the sunrise, and four distinctly different kingdoms maintain control.

Calabiyau Proper: The Kingdom of the Fée

The Biyau family (Kandide's lineage) has ruled Calabiyau Proper since the Year of the Fée, 08 BT (beginning of time). In the year 26,804 BT, the High Council, consisting of twelve elected representatives from the twelve primary faery clans, signed a treaty with King Toeyad to participate in the governing of their land.

Calabiyau West: The Kingdom of the Banshees

When precious gems were discovered in the Year of the Fée 808 BT, the Banshee clans split off from the other Fée and formed their own separatist kingdom. Since that time, hundreds of different monarchs have ruled over the Banshees. In the Year of the Fée 26,449 BT, King Nastae assumed the throne.

Calabiyau East: The Veil of the Mists

Founded in the Year of the Fée 26,851 BT, the Veil is presided over by Selena as an independent, democratically governed territory. It is surrounded by a dark and terrifying area known as the Mists.

Calabiyau North: The Bardic Council

Founded in 12,247 BT and presided over by High Priestess Viviana, this secretive land is home to wizards and bards. It is almost impossible to get to, and few even know of its existence.

CALABIYAU

'Tis not so long ago, nor so far away, but indeed a time and place quite near, if only we would see.

Some call it an enchanted realm, others say it is the elemental dimension, and still others simply call it faery land.

Long written about by scholars, long over-looked by all but those with acute perception, this world is no less real, and its reality is of no less consequence.

PROLOGUE

King Toeyad had only enough time to catch a glimpse of the deadly arrow that pointed directly toward him. Although he was standing a good fifty meters away, he did not question that its aim would be precise. Barely hearing the distinctive rush of air that signified the lethal projectile's release, the king fell to the ground. The razor-sharp tip had struck its intended mark. A piercing scream rang out. Kandide, still holding her crossbow, rushed to his side.

ONE

"Where . . . where am I?" Kandide spoke in little more than a whisper. Her purple-blue eyes darted from tree to tree as she nervously scanned the lifeless forest. "What . . . what is this place?"

Nothing was as it should be. Dense black fog shrouded the gnarled trees, blocking all but the most persistent rays of sun. The ground was marshy and slick beneath Kandide's feet, and her nostrils stung with the acidic smell of rotting death. There was an uncanny sense of quiet—too quiet. Not even the chirping of a woodland bird could be heard. It was as though someone or something had scared every living creature away.

"Is nothing here alive?" she whispered. This time it was more to hear herself speak than an expectation that anyone would answer. "How . . . how could Mother have sent me here?"

It was on that very morning that Kandide was to be crowned Queen of Calabiyau Proper, the kingdom of the Fée. The last thing she remembered was speaking to her subjects from the grand balcony of the Imperial Castle. Then, with a sudden gesture of her mother's hand, she was instantly standing alone in this bleak, shadowy land.

Still wearing her pearlescent cape and the formal attire of the court, the Fée princess could not have been more inappropriately dressed.

The hem of her long, flowing gown was already laced with black mud. Its delicate fabric seemed to snag on the dense underbrush with every step she took. And yet, even in her distress, Kandide was poised and beautiful beyond compare. She had the proud look of nobility. With high cheekbones and skin that was silvery-white like freshly fallen snow, her nearly waist-length hair shimmered gold one minute and platinum the next.

Careful not to slip on the slimy ground, she cautiously looked around, trying to establish some sort of bearing—a landmark, something that would tell her where she was. But there were no landmarks, only thick, tangled vines hanging from dead tree branches that seemed to reach out and claw at her as she tried to make her way through. To what? She did not know. To where? That Kandide knew not either.

After daring to take a few more steps, she was suddenly halted. Her head jerked violently backwards. Frozen in her tracks, Kandide felt her heart begin to pound. She could not move. She was afraid to breathe.

Slowly, she looked up. But there was nothing to see—nothing

KANDIDE

except the twisted branch that caught in her hair. Snapping it in two, she hastily freed herself from its thorny grasp.

As she stood there pulling each splintered piece of wood from her long golden braid, anger started to set in—anger at her mother for sending her there, anger at her sister, Tara, for not doing more to help her, and anger at the court healers—especially at the court healers. Each time she moved her left arm, a sharp pain shot through her shoulder and wing. It was a constant reminder of the terrible accident and how her finest healers just stood there doing nothing to help her. *They didn't even try,* she thought, tossing the last sliver of bark to the ground. *They're jealous. They're all jealous of my beauty, that's why.*

With each step she took, Kandide's annoyance increased, as did her overwhelming sense of helplessness. She was disoriented, exhausted, and completely alone, perhaps for the first time in her life. Panic began to replace common sense. Her anger quickly gave way to all of the other emotions that she had kept pent up for so very long. The pain. The fear. The guilt. The shame. The sadness—the terrible sadness over losing her father—all of these emotions seemed to consume her at once.

Mother sent me away. Why does she hate me so? Tears began to well up in her eyes. *It wasn't my fault. Mother blames me, that's why. Now she hates me—they all hate me because I'm ... I'm ... an Imperf—*

"Nooo!" Kandide shrieked, desperately trying to maintain some semblance of control. "I ... I must think ... think only about what to do right now. I must not think about Mother, or Tara, or the healers—only about what to do. If only I had my crossbow, at least then . . ." With a few deep breaths, Kandide began to regain her composure. Her father's words returned: "Strength and courage are what matter most when times are not as we wish, my daughter," he reminded her as he lay dying.

"Strength and courage—that's it! Strength and courage." Under her breath, Kandide repeated his words, over and over again. "Strength and courage. Strength and courage. Strength and courage."

She swallowed hard, determined to transform her panic into purpose. Kandide knew that she must quickly find a way out of this horrific place. "There has to be a path or something—and I will find it. I always do."

Kandide began making her way, albeit slowly, through the thick underbrush. With each step she took, black mud oozed through her open-toed slippers, almost causing one to be lost in the gooey muck. Nevertheless, she forced herself to keep pressing onward.

For over an hour, she persevered, constantly searching for some type of identifiable landmark. With the sun almost completely obscured by the heavy fog, maintaining any sort of direction was nearly impossible. The small strips of cloth that she tore from her numerous under-slips and tied to every third tree kept her from going in circles. But they did nothing to stop her from going deeper and deeper into the shadowy forest.

Pausing for a moment to rest, Kandide suddenly spotted a small cavelike structure only a few meters ahead. It wasn't much—just a few massive boulders piled one on top of the other. But with the woods getting darker by the minute, it was probably her best hope of finding at least some sort of shelter. Maybe her only hope.

Perhaps I should rest here, she thought as she cautiously made her way over to the crude refuge and peered inside. *It looks empty enough.* Not sure what else to do, Kandide ducked her head and went in. *It has to be safer than trying to find my way out of this place in the dark.*

Although winter had not yet set in, the fog-laden air was chilly and damp, and she was glad to have at least some sort of shelter. *Yes, I shall stay here until morning,* she thought as she settled down on a flat rock that protruded from the ground near the cave's back wall. It was a far cry from her own luxuriously appointed bedchamber with its cozy warm comforter and soft satin sheets, but at least for this night, it would have to do.

Kandide pulled her cape tightly around her shoulders, desperately trying to ward off the extreme cold she suddenly felt. Her shoulder and wing throbbed with pain, and her stomach rumbled. She couldn't even remember the last time she had eaten a meal.

Although exhausted and scared, she was determined not to let her emotions take control. She thought of her family and the events that led up to her being sent away. If only her sister, Tara, hadn't agreed to go to the meadows. If only her brother, Teren, hadn't created that silly spell. If only her father hadn't . . . if . . . if . . . if . . .

Kandide blinked back a tear, once again thinking of her father. "*If* could put a thousand hectares in a bottle," the great king would say when she tried to use "if" as an excuse to justify her almost always self-centered actions. She could not help but smile at the wisdom of his neverending counsel. "*If* is a master you must not serve, my child," he would gently admonish, "for it will only hinder your ambition, not enable your task."

Still smiling, Kandide rubbed her hands together in a slow circular motion, and a small bluish light appeared between her fingertips.

She uttered a magical phrase: "From flame to light, now grow, be bright. I command you this moment, to enable my sight." As she spoke, the tiny blue orb grew larger and larger. She placed the softly glowing light on a flat recess above her head. It was just bright enough to illuminate her small shelter. *At least my little brother is of some use,* she thought. *Guess I'll have to thank him for teaching me that trick—if I ever see him again.*

Cold, hungry, and alone, Kandide could not help but think about all that had happened. Her thoughts drifted back to when everything began to change. It was the worst four days of her life . . .

"Exceptional talent does not justify exceptional selfishness."

TWO

"It isn't that Kandide means to be unkind, my love," King Toeyad whispered to his beloved wife, Queen Tiyana. "She has simply been raised to be queen."

"She has been raised to think that the world, including you, should indulge her every whim." Tiyana lovingly placed her hand on her husband's cheek. "Oh why, my darling, why did you have to play that deadly archery game with Kandide? Why now?"

"It was to be my final lesson to her," he softly replied. It took a great deal of effort for him to do so, but he reached up to hold her hand.

King Toeyad and Queen Tiyana ruled over Calabiyau Proper. It was Toeyad's long-ago ancestors for whom this land was named. The Biyau family, of the Water Clan, had been the sovereign monarchs since the Year of the Fée, 08 BT (beginning of time). When the family assumed control, the word *cala*, meaning "land" in the language of the ancients, was added to their own name—hence Calabiyau, land of Biyau.

Toeyad had been king of this enchanted land for nearly four hundred years. And while it is not uncommon for Fée to live a half a millennium or more, no one but the eldest of the elders could remember a time when he did not rule. Many considered him to be their greatest leader. Certainly, history would reveal him to be one of their wisest and most beloved. Princess Kandide was the eldest of his three children, and, therefore, first in line to inherit the throne upon his passing.

From his richly carved canopied bed with its deep purple satin sheets and overstuffed pillows, the dying king looked up at Tiyana with a reassuring smile. "Kandide will have many battles to face as queen. She must truly know, not just in her head, but deep within her heart, that lives are dependent upon her skill and expertise."

"Just as your life was during that game," Tiyana asserted.

"Just as my life would have been had her skill with a crossbow not been so great. For as you well know, it was not Kandide's arrow that caused my collapse."

"That is my point, exactly." Frustrated with her daughter's behavior, Tiyana shook her head. "Knowing that you are in failing health, she should not have kept you out there for so long."

"If only you could have seen her, Tiyana. Kandide played with the skill of an absolute master. Her arrows struck my gaming shield twenty-six times—each a perfect center hit." Although Toeyad's strength was fading, he seemed to be invigorated at the thought of how well his daughter had played. "That kind of score simply does not happen in this game."

"Exceptional talent does not justify exceptional selfishness. And it certainly does not excuse Kandide's behavior now, disappearing like this."

"As usual, my love, you are right on both accounts."

"And as usual, my darling king, you chose not to deny her— on twenty-six accounts!"

"Just as I could never deny you, my beloved, on any account." Looking at her with a flirtatious grin, Toeyad softly kissed his wife's hand.

He may be weak, but Tiyana still found his smile irresistible. Only slightly reprimanding him for his words, she added, "I wouldn't mind your indulging her so, if Kandide actually learned some of the lessons that you attempt to teach her. Even now, with all that is happening, she continues to think only of herself."

"All of her life she has been told how very special she is. How very beautiful. How very perfect."

"How very spoiled!" On this Tiyana would not relent.

"Kandide is young and has not yet realized that her authority must be tempered with reverence. But worry not, my love, it will come. Age does find wisdom, you know."

"We can only hope." Tiyana's sigh revealed that she was not at all convinced that their eldest daughter would ever be anything but completely spoiled and self-centered.

"After all," King Toeyad insisted with a loving smile, "she carries your essence as well as mine. And you, my queen, are the personification of regard. Please send her to me as soon as she is found. I fear I have very little time left. The fates will not be denied much longer. I must transfer the Gift to Kandide before my strength completely fails. As you well know, all life depends upon it."

"I shall do my very best." Tiyana's frustration could not have been more apparent. "Who knows where that girl might be?"

Reports of King Toeyad's imminent passing quickly spread throughout the land. Greatly saddened by the news, the Fée, out of deep respect, had all but stopped their daily activities. Bread ovens began to cool from fires not stoked, pumpkins and crooked-neck yellow squash lay unharvested in the fields, and shops of every kind stood empty as most villagers waited in the central square for some sort of message about their beloved king. It was as though all in Calabiyau were holding their breath, awaiting word—all but Princess Kandide, that is.

She had simply vanished.

THREE

"Well, she's not in the meadows!" Prince Teren exclaimed as he swooped into the king's chamber.

Having just reached his fourteenth birthday, Teren was the youngest of their three children and their only son. Although he looked exactly like Toeyad had when he was young, with the same roguish smile, high forehead, yellow-brown eyes, and tousled sandy-blond hair, that was where the similarity ended.

Known more for his practical jokes than his princely manner, Teren's primary goal in life was to become a great and mighty magi—a worker of wonders who could conjure up wizardly enchantments. He was often found in the Royal Library with his nose buried in an ancient book on magic or spell weaving. That is, when he wasn't devising some sort of a mischievous prank, something he enjoyed almost as much as learning a new bit of wizardry.

The legendary Merlin was Teren's idol. Drawings and books of the great wizard could be found scattered all about his bedchamber.

"I'll go look for her some more, if you want me to, Mother," the young prince offered. "Hey, maybe she went to that little chocolate shop down in the village that she likes so much. You know, the one where she always goes when she feels sorry for herself. I could look there, or maybe—"

"No, Teren, you stay here with your father. I shall go look for her myself. Perhaps I will have better luck." Tiyana was suddenly struck by a thought. She looked at her son a bit askance. "You didn't put one of your spells on Kandide, did you? That's not why she is missing, is it?"

"Mother! Would I do tha—?"

"It has been known to happen. In any case, I want you to stay here and spend some time with your father." Attempting a smile, Tiyana's face revealed only anguish at the thought of leaving her beloved Toeyad's side, even for a few minutes. But Kandide must be found, and soon.

"Worry not, my love," the great king reassured her. "As you can see, I am actually feeling a bit stronger just now. Find Kandide. The Gift must be transferred to her while I am still able."

Even in his gravely weakened state, King Toeyad was more commanding than anyone Tiyana had ever known. His hair had silvered and his body was surely fading, but he still exuded a presence and authority that was simply unequaled. And while Toeyad may not have been the most handsome of the Fée,

PRINCE TEREN

to this day, he had a reassuring smile that simply melted hearts.

"I shall not pass before you return," he insisted with the same confident look that made Tiyana fall in love with him so many years ago.

"You had better not." Turning to depart, Tiyana briefly paused to look back at her husband. She forced a smile, and then looked straight at her son. "And you had better make sure of it!"

"I will, Mother!" Teren called after her as she reluctantly departed to search for Kandide. "I'll make sure."

*"A secret?" Teren's eyes lit up.
"Yes, a secret."*

FOUR

King Toeyad's bedchamber was dimly lit, reflecting the somber mood that prevailed throughout the castle. The subtle fragrance of violet oil filled the air, and the softly glowing embers inside his ancient flagstone fireplace were barely burning. Even the sky seemed saddened, wrapped in its dull gray shroud as though it was just waiting to burst forth with the tears that the king's passing would bring. Throughout the castle, forlorn faces replaced the gaiety of happier times. Only Toeyad seemed not to be sorrowful. Despite his weakened body, he had a smile and positive word for each who entered his room.

"I'm happy you are here, Teren," the king whispered with a nod. "I have not been able to spend enough time with you over these recent weeks, and for that I apologize."

"It's okay, Father. I understand. We're together now."

Trying to think of something to say to conceal his immense sadness, Teren looked around the chamber and quickly remarked, "It's kind of dark in here, don't you think? Should I open the curtains?"

"Yes, I'd like that. I don't know why everyone insists upon closing them."

Hesitating, Teren looked back at his father. "Are you sure it's okay?"

"I am still king, Teren. I assure you, it is okay."

As he pulled open the drapes, the young prince continued, "Are you really feeling better, Father?"

"A little. Now, I have a question for you—and I want you to be truthful with me. You didn't turn Kandide into a frog or anything, did you?"

"Of course not!" Teren hastily pulled back the deep purple and gold brocade curtains, then walked over and sat down on the neatly upholstered purple and gold chair next to his father's massive bed. "Besides, I haven't gotten that one to work right yet."

"You're quite sure?"

"I'm sure! Hey, remember the time I put a spell on Kandide so that she'd sneeze every time she looked in the mirror?"

"I remember that she sneezed almost constantly for three weeks, until your little spell finally wore off."

"That was one of my best ones!" Teren started to giggle. "Gosh, Kandide's vain."

Toeyad also started to chuckle at the memory of his son's prank. "I don't think Kandide thought it was very funny. And you didn't do much laughing, either, when you found out that you would be spending the next two weeks confined to your bedchamber."

"That was the part that wasn't funny." Teren was still giggling. "Anyway, I think I've finally figured out how to undo my spells. Tara and me have been working on it."

"Tara and I." Toeyad might have been weak, but he would go to his passing trying to get his son to use correct grammar.

"Sorry, Father—Tara and I." Teren suddenly noticed a serving Fée who had entered the room. Her arms were wrapped around a huge bouquet of brightly colored tiger lilies, which she artfully arranged in a large golden vase. Looking at her, a mischievous thought crossed Teren's mind. "Want me to show you how it works?"

"Absolutely not!" Toeyad acknowledged the Fée with a nod and a smile of thanks. She graciously curtsied to the king, and then promptly exited, knowing all too well of Teren's mischievous spells.

With a great deal of effort, King Toeyad reached over and patted his son's hand, commenting, "I am, however, quite pleased to hear that you are making progress with your lessons. Would you like to learn a secret?"

"A secret?" Teren's eyes lit up.

"Yes, a secret. I was known to weave a few good-natured spells myself when I was your age."

"You, Father? You never told me that. Did you really? Tell me about one. Please . . . please, Father?"

"Only if you promise not to try doing it—at least, not until you've practiced," he quickly added, seeing the overly eager look on his son's face.

"I promise! I promise!"

"Then help me to sit up and I will tell you about it." Although it was difficult for him, Toeyad leaned forward, holding on to his son's arm while Teren placed several large, fluffy pillows behind his back and head.

Suddenly realizing how weak his father really was, Teren's excited expression transformed to one of great concern. "Are you . . . are you sure you're okay, Father?"

"I'm okay, Teren. Now, listen closely. There was an old wizard named Melini. Max, we used to call him. He was the most amazing wizard I have ever known. Rumor had it that he was related to Merlin."

"Really? To Merlin?"

"Indeed. He taught me a spell that I think you may find quite handy . . ."

FIVE

"Where could your sister possibly be?" Queen Tiyana was speaking to her youngest daughter, Princess Tara, as the two of them reentered King Toeyad's antechamber. "I fear that your father is far weaker than he will admit. Kandide knows that his time with us grows perilously short."

Tara looked up at her mother. Her eyes were full of tears. "I wish there was something I could do for Father."

"I know, my child. I know. But there is nothing any of us can do—except to be with him now. Your sister is so self-cent—"

"That's just Kandi, Mother. You know how she is."

Princess Tara was the only one permitted to call her sister "Kandi." It was an endearment that the crown princess had allowed Tara from the time she first started speaking and couldn't quite pronounce Kandide. Even Teren faced the future queen's wrath should he call her as such.

"She simply does everything on her own time," Tara shrugged.

"And in her own way. Blessed be, I think your sister gets more self-centered with every season."

"Your Majesty!" Mylea, Kandide's number one lady-in-waiting, came rushing into the room. "We have finally located Princess Kandide!"

Tiyana and Tara turned to acknowledge the anxious Fée. "Thank the earthly spirits. Where is she?" Tiyana questioned.

Curtseying to the queen, Mylea explained, "Her Royal Highness has just now returned to her chamber from the gaming fields."

"Of course, I should have thought to look there." Tiyana was glib in her response. "Her father is close to passing and Kandide is out practicing games of skill. Why does that not surprise me? Please, Mylea, send her to me, immediately."

Mylea stared awkwardly at the floor while incessantly wringing her hands. She looked up only slightly to deliver Kandide's excuse. "I have tried, Your Majesty, but she says she must finish braiding her hair and will yet be a while."

"May the earthly spirits help us when that girl is crowned!"

"Now, Mother, you know how Kandi is about looking perfect." True to her nature, Tara once again attempted to minimize her sister's unfathomable behavior. "Let me go and see if I can hasten her."

Princess Tara was the antithesis of Kandide. Unselfish, gracious, and loving, she was as dutiful as any daughter could possibly be, but then she had not been raised to be queen.

PRINCESS TARA

The young princess spent much of her time helping others—that is, when she wasn't defending Kandide for one of her arrogant comments or self-centered deeds. It was something her sister seemed to be doing a great deal more of since their father had become ill.

Humble and bright, Tara was sweet and kind. Except for her green eyes, she looked like her mother, with deep auburn hair and pale-green skin. A bit more elfin in nature, Tara preferred to wear britches and boots, and, unlike Kandide, was almost never seen in the more formal attire of the court. She wanted nothing to do with ruling the Fée or with faery politics of any kind, and was perfectly happy knowing that Kandide would assume that role.

*Before Tiyana could wipe the tears away,
the antechamber doors burst open.*

SIX

Healing was Tara's Gift and, more than anything, she loved to spend her free time in the forest helping injured animals. But even with her extraordinary Talent, the young princess could not heal her father. It was simply his time to pass.

Tara had received the Gift of Healing when she was a small child, from her late Aunt Selena, Tiyana's identical twin. The sisters were so very close and so very much alike that there were times when even King Toeyad could not tell the two of them apart. Selena's sudden and untimely passing, when Tara was not yet four, brought profound sorrow throughout the kingdom, for she was also dearly loved and respected for her kind, unselfish ways.

It is the irony of the Fée that, no matter how strong their Talent, they cannot heal themselves. Their energy simply cannot be channeled back through their own bodies. Sadly, Selena's injuries were so severe that none of the other healers were able to help her, even when several tried linking their Talents together. Knowing that her amazing Talent would be lost, Selena transferred it to Tara, and the young princess grew to become one of the most powerful healers in all the land.

As Tara rushed off to hasten Kandide, Tiyana sat down on the soft, oversized love seat where she and her beloved husband had shared so many quiet conversations. *How Toeyad loves purple,* she thought, as she gazed around at the color scheme of his antechamber. *I guess he would have painted the entire castle as such, if he were allowed. Maybe the entire village!* The thought of purple thatched roofs almost made her chuckle.

On this day, Tiyana was wearing Toeyad's favorite gown. It, too, was purple. Delicate lavender lace framed her face, as tiny folds of deep royal purple velvet, tightly gathered around her waist, accentuated her still-perfect figure. Long, graceful sleeves almost covered her hands. She was also wearing the amethyst, diamond, and imperial topaz collar necklace that Toeyad designed for her upon their engagement. It was without question her favorite piece of jewelry.

A saddened smile crossed Tiyana's face as she fought back her overwhelming sorrow. She was well aware that, while the fates may sometimes be altered, passing is destiny's one undeniable claim on all of life's creatures.

Tiyana and Toeyad had ruled together for well over a century, and yet, to her, it seemed like only yesterday that they were first united. "Where has the time gone, my beloved?" she whispered to herself. Looking at her own long auburn curls in the large gilded mirror that adorned most of the end wall of the King's antechamber, Tiyana sighed. "And where did all of these silver streaks come from?" Piled atop her head, curls randomly spilled over her diamond and amethyst-encrusted tiara, the one Toeyad had presented to her on the day he made her his queen.

"Time only enhances your beauty," he would say when she fretted about the fact that even the Fée must age, albeit far more slowly than humankind.

Tiyana's thoughts drifted back to the time when Toeyad first swept her off her feet. She was not yet twenty-five years of age. His endearing smile had never stopped sending tingles throughout her body.

"I have searched three centuries to find you, my dear," Toeyad proclaimed to Tiyana shortly after their first meeting, "but it took less than an instant to fall in love with you." From their first encounter in Tiyana's tiny forest village with its oddly shaped thatched roofs, the great king knew it was his destiny to have Tiyana rule by his side.

For a few fleeting moments, she also remembered the seldom and oh-so-precious carefree times that they shared when, together, they would fly off into the woods, or tumble over laughing as they gathered sunbeams in the meadows. On one very special day, Toeyad wove the brightest ones into a crown that he fashioned out of freshly gathered flowers. Placing it on Tiyana's head, he stood back and looked at her.

Then, with a deep frown, he shook his head from side to side, commenting, "No, no matter how hard I try, nothing can outshine your beauty, my love." The two of them laughed, swooping off to gather wild honey and fresh berries.

In all the world, could there ever be a kinder, more wonderful Fée? Again, looking into the mirror, she tried to blink back the tears that kept welling up in her purple-blue eyes. Could not Kandide have gotten some of his essence?

Before Tiyana could wipe the tears away, the antechamber doors burst open.

SEVEN

"**M**other, what do you mean sending Tara to hasten me?" an irate Princess Kandide blurted out in a manner that was totally devoid of any feelings other than her own.

Thrust back into reality, Tiyana quickly stood up. "Kandide, I asked you to stay near. You know your father does not have the strength to deploy the Gift. It must be transferred to you immediately."

"Can't it wait just a few minutes longer, Mother? I haven't finished my braid." Kandide's tone was not at all contemptuous, only such that it made no sense to her that her father should pass, at least not until she looked her very best.

"I fear, my daughter, that even you cannot control your father's passing."

"But you know I must look perfect for him—especially now!"

Perfection is important to the Fée. To Kandide, it was an obsession. While it is true that each clan measures perfection differently—some clans are tall, some are short, some are green, and others are dark or light—all have unwavering standards that are used to judge an individual's worth and status.

Dressed in an off-white iridescent cape that seemed to change color with each movement, Kandide was, indeed, the personification of perfection in spite of her still unfinished braid. Tall and statuesque, she was also perfectly beautiful—a combination that the Fée prize above all else.

"Besides," the crown princess attempted to rationalize her tardiness, "I am told that Father is feeling stronger. Perhaps he—"

"No, Kandide. Your father's renewed strength is only the natural occurrence that often happens just prior to the passing. I fear it is an indication that his time is very near." On this day, Tiyana had no patience for her daughter's self-centered ways. "Now, stop thinking only of yourself and join me in his chamber this instant. For once, you must face reality, child. You may be the next queen, but you are Toeyad's daughter first, and that means showing respect."

With the defiant poise of a captive snow leopard, the crown princess grudgingly acquiesced. "Yes, Mother."

Nodding her head in the slightest of bows, Kandide followed Tiyana into her father's bedchamber. Tara and Teren were already by his side.

EIGHT

Kandide seldom showed emotion. After all, "Leaders simply don't do as such," she would say.

Seeing her father so very translucent, so very close to passing, however, was more than even she could bear. A tear rolled down her cheek. She tried to compose herself. *No, I will not cry. I am King Toeyad's daughter, heir to the throne, and the very essence of his being. Because of him, I am strong.* Kandide hastily assumed her place at his bedside.

Reaching up to wipe away the tear, King Toeyad softly spoke. "You must remember your destiny, my child. Strength and courage are what matter when times are not as we wish."

"But, Father, I do not wish you to pass." Kandide spoke as though her very words could alter his fate.

"Hush now, my daughter. All seasons must change. To live is also to pass, for only then can the cycle start anew. I have raised you to take my place—to be a great leader, and that you must be."

Kandide could do no wrong in Toeyad's eyes. The only thing that he and Tiyana ever argued about was how to raise her. "Self-confidence is good," he would say when she was being particularly arrogant. "After all, she will have many challenges to face as queen."

It was King Toeyad who pampered and spoiled Kandide so. He simply could not say no to those exquisite purple-blue eyes. Even in his last moments, Kandide's tardy behavior did not alter his ability to see the good in her. Not that it could, for Toeyad saw the good in all creatures, even, to Kandide's abhorrence, the Imperfects, those Fée who are not physically perfect due to a deformity or permanent injury. When given the chance, he would insist upon championing their cause at the High Council meetings. It was something Kandide never quite understood, for her own perception of beauty was entirely wrapped around physical perfection.

In spite of his indulgence, King Toeyad also taught his eldest daughter to be remarkably courageous and self-reliant. Not only did he make sure that she was extremely well educated and a superb archer, but also well trained in other battle games as well. So, regardless of Kandide's wishing on this day, Toeyad's passing was truly to be his final lesson to her—one of strength, courage, and self-reliance. For this lesson, however, there would be only his memory to continue her guidance.

"Rule with strength and courage, my child," he whispered, taking her hand. "And always with a kind and accepting heart, for each determines destiny. The power of the throne, as well as the Gift, will soon be yours. They both have the ability to change the world—for better or for worse."

A deep pout crossed Kandide's otherwise exquisite face. "Yes, Father."

"Before I transfer the Gift, I must also give you this." Toeyad handed Kandide a simple white feather with a thin silver band spiraled around its quill.

She looked at it rather quizzically, and her father explained: "Is it not the simple feather that allows eagles to soar, that protects waterfowl from freezing, or that, with a stroke of its quill, has altered destiny? Learn to look beneath the surface, my child. Remember, truth, like strength, often lies where least expected."

"But I—"

"Always keep this small reminder near. It will serve you well."

"As you wish, Father." Having no idea what he meant, she took the feather and carefully placed it in the pocket of her cape.

"And now you must ready yourself to accept the Gift, my child."

"I am ready, Father."

Kandide gasped for air. Perspiration streamed down her forehead, and her breathing became more and more erratic.

NINE

Toeyad reached out to place his hands against Kandide's. Looking up at her, he asked, "Do you willingly accept this Gift, my daughter?"

"Yes, Father," she nodded.

"Do you understand its true power and importance to all creatures of our great planet?"

"Yes, Father."

"Do you willingly agree to be the guardian of the Gift, placing its care even above your own life?"

"Yes, Father."

"Are you ready then for the transfer, my daughter?"

"I am, Father."

With a precise rhythm, first the index fingers on each of their hands touched, and then their middle, ring, and little fingers. Finally, their thumbs joined, sparking a powerful electrical current that began wildly arcing from Toeyad to Kandide. She could feel the immense power surging into her body. It filled every fiber of her being with intense feelings that ranged from euphoria to excruciating pain. The force of the current steadily increased—each new jolt becoming more powerful and more unbearable than the last. Kandide struggled to breathe.

And so the transfer of that most precious and crucial of all gifts, the Gift of the Frost, had begun—for it is the deploying of the frost that provokes the atmospheric instabilities that create winter's icy precipitation. Without this provocation, Mother Nature's miracles of birth and rebirth could simply not transpire. The leaves could not fall, winter could not settle in, and spring could not bring forth a new beginning. All life would soon begin to die.

Since the beginning of time, generation after generation of King Toeyad's family had deployed the Gift. Now, it was to be Kandide's turn, and she was to be its sole keeper.

As the transfer continued, Kandide began shaking so violently that she almost lost consciousness. She gasped for air. Perspiration streamed down her forehead, and her breathing became more and more erratic. Her father had warned her of this, but the seemingly endless jolts from such a tremendous energy transfer were far worse than she could have ever imagined. This, however, was something she had to endure. *Endure it, I will*, she thought, fighting back the awful pain. It was all she could do to keep from going into shock. By now, the force had become so strong that her entire body was engulfed in a glistening iridescent halo of pure electrical current.

As suddenly as they started, the agonizing jolts abruptly stopped. Kandide was dripping wet. Numb, she slowly began to relax as the dreadful spasms subsided.

Virtually drained of the Gift, Toeyad was, at last, able to separate his hands from hers. Falling back onto the overstuffed pillows that had been supporting him, the king was breathing so heavily that he was only able to speak in short, strained phrases. "You must now . . . finish . . . my work . . . Kandide," he gasped, inhaling deeply several more times before attempting to speak again.

With the enormous power of her newly acquired gift, Kandide's breathing quickly returned to normal. Most remarkably, she was no longer exhausted and felt more alive than ever before. Barely hearing her father's words, she stood up and gazed at her own glorious reflection in his large chamber mirror. Blotting the last few beads of perspiration from her forehead, Kandide simply could not help but admire how very beautiful she looked. With the energy from the Gift, she radiated a magnificent silvery glow, causing her extraordinary beauty to become even more resplendent.

"Use the Gift . . . and . . . the throne . . . wisely, my daughter," Toeyad continued. He was still only able to speak in quick breaths. "You must . . . become the leader of *all* Fée. Only then . . . will you have earned your right . . . to be the true queen."

More interested in her own appearance than her father's prophetic counsel, Kandide half-heartedly responded to his comments. "Yes, Father . . . Father!" Suddenly, snapped back to the reality of the moment, she quickly knelt down beside him. Tenderly kissing him on both cheeks, Kandide softly whispered, "I love you, Father. I am so sorry that I did this to you. I never meant to keep you out there so long. I love you so very much."

"And I love you, Kandide." He looked deeply into her tearful eyes. "I chose . . . my destiny, not you, my daughter. Your actions . . . did not alter the fates. Of my time . . . for passing, even you have no control. Remember . . . my words—all . . . of them."

"I will, Father."

"Good. Now I must speak . . . to your brother and sister." With one last reassuring nod, Toeyad smiled at his eldest daughter. She reluctantly left his side. Walking over to her mother, Kandide struggled to keep from sobbing uncontrollably. *I will not cry. I am Toeyad's daughter,* she kept repeating to herself. *I am Toeyad's daughter . . . heir to the throne. I will not cry. I must not be weak.*

After beckoning Tara and Teren to come sit by his side, their father whispered, "Take care of Kandide, my children, for the two of you . . . are also written in the fates. She may be older, but . . . you, Tara, are wiser, with far greater . . . perception. Kandide needs your compassion and . . . gentle spirit. And you, Teren, she needs your humor, optimism, and that . . . remarkably clever and determined . . . mind. Both of you will ultimately help her . . . along her path . . . of serving *all* Fée. Only then . . . will each of you be free to pursue your individual destinies."

"Us? Help Kandide?" Teren was completely baffled by his father's words. Kandide rarely accepted help from anyone, especially him.

"How?" Tara looked at her father with a bewildered expression.

"I do not know how, but ... guide your sister well. She needs you both, more ... than any of us can ever know."

As confusing as her father's request was, Tara promised, "Although I do not know how, I will, of course, do as you ask, Father." Tears streamed down her face. She simply could not contain her sorrow.

"Me, too, Father," Teren pledged.

"Don't be sad, either of you. I have lived a good ... and long life, and the two of you have been so very much ... a part of my joy. Carry with you at all times ... the undying love, determination, and respect of your father. This is my parting gift to you both."

"No greater gift could we want," Tara answered, trying to blink back her tears. "Know that you also carry my undying love and respect."

"It is a father's honor ... to be told that by his daughter," he whispered with one last gentle squeeze of her hand. "Now it is time for me ... to speak to your mother."

"I love you too, Father," Teren added, turning away so that his father would not see him cry. After all, he was his father's son and well on his way to becoming a great and powerful magi. *I won't cry,* he thought, while wiping a tear away with his sleeve.

Turning to Tiyana, Toeyad humbly made one last request of her as well. "My beloved queen, no one ... has ever had a better partner ... than I. You, and you alone, provided me with unyielding strength ... when my own resolve would begin to falter. My accomplishments ... are equally your accomplishments. Together, we ... have altered destiny. Will you ... do me the great honor of accepting ... my last kiss?"

Tiyana's heart sank as her thoughts adjusted to the inevitable reality of the moment, for that kiss would, indeed, be his last. Kneeling beside him, their lips met and she, too, became surrounded by a glowing radiance. Toeyad's final kiss was offered so that a small portion of his essence would always remain within her. Among the Fée, it is the ultimate gift, the Gift of Everlasting Love.

It was also his final gift. Only the fading glow of Toeyad's body remained where once lay Tiyana's most mighty love and the greatest ruler the Fée had ever known. His passing was complete. He was forever gone from her side. Having watched life's illuminating power vanish from her beloved husband, Tiyana simply could not contain her sorrow. Her thoughts were lost in her memories as she tried in vain to fight back the ever-increasing flood of tears.

His very being had returned to the eternal tributary from which all life flows, and ultimately to which all life must return. Perhaps, she could only hope, they would meet again along another point in the ever-revolving cycles of time.

Tiyana and her three children slowly left his chamber. Momentarily turning back, she softly whispered, "Good-bye, my beloved. Good-bye."

TEN

In an attempt to remember happier times, Tiyana settled into an overstuffed chair in her private antechamber. Unlike Toeyad, who loved everything purple, her rooms were decorated in the lush greens of the forest. It reminded her of the woods where she and Selena grew up. Sitting there, alone, Tiyana thought about all she and Toeyad had achieved during their rule together.

As little as a hundred years ago, things were very different for the Fée. Calabiyau was in constant turmoil, and the clans by no means lived in harmony. Although King Toeyad's family had ruled this land almost since the beginning of time, jealousy, arrogance, and struggles for power dominated faery politics for as long as anyone could remember. Had his ancestors not possessed the Gift, they surely would have been dethroned millennia ago. Each clan considered itself to be more important than the next, and even the minutest of differences would often end up in terrible clashes, if not all-out battles.

It was only due to Toeyad's great vision and skill as a leader that the clans were finally united. His father before him had tried to stop the fighting, and his father before him, and before him—each to no avail. But Toeyad's commanding presence, combined with his unwavering persistence and skill in negotiating the Treaty, eventually paid off. He achieved what most thought impossible. He united the various faery clans, and, for most of the past century, all had lived in harmony.

All, that is, except the Banshees, who, under the pretense of protecting their vast hordes of gold and precious gems, remained extremely hostile. Banshees love jewels beyond all else. It was told that they had enormous stashes of diamonds, emeralds, rubies, and sapphires hidden within their secret network of caves. It was also told that they bred hideous creatures called garglans to protect their treasures.

With all of his skill and persuasion, King Toeyad was unable to bring the Banshees into the High Council. Their highly volatile and fierce warlike nature simply would not allow it to be. The best he could do was to negotiate a truce with their leader, King Nastae, to not invade the other clans. Except for the occasional attack by small outlaw bands of Banshee renegades, the Treaty was, for the most part, upheld.

Tiyana was certain that King Nastae was behind these brutal raids, but neither she nor King Toeyad could prove it. Even thinking about the horrible atrocities they committed, for no apparent reason other than to terrorize the bordering villages, made Tiyana quiver.

We've come a long way, my love, she thought, *but there is still so much more to do. I only hope Kandide is able to finish your work and create a true peace with the Banshees.*

As she thought about their extraordinary life together, Tiyana's eyes once again filled with tears. For her, there would be only memories—only the past to keep her love alive. Knowing that all life must pass—her own, one day, as well—was small comfort for the emptiness she felt. Tears streamed down her cheeks as she thought about never seeing her beloved Toeyad smile again, never hearing his laugh, never feeling his touch. She knew it was selfish of her, but when it came to Toeyad, Tiyana could never be selfish enough.

His was the gentle commanding strength that inspired legends, and theirs was a love that the bards would forever sing about . . .

> *They ruled the Fée, with head and heart,*
> *and gave each clan a bright new start.*
> *To see them smile, to see them care,*
> *is to see the world without despair.*
> *To know the love they shared together,*
> *is to know the world is forever better.*
> *To see them smile, to see them care,*
> *is to see the world without despair.*

In her heart, Tiyana could not help but ache for the past. In her head, however, she knew that she must begin to focus on the future. Reaching up to turn off the oil lamp that softly illuminated her chamber, she whispered, "Good night, my love. Good night."

ELEVEN

Word of King Toeyad's passing quickly spread throughout the clans. Not a crop was picked nor shop left open as all paused to say good-bye. Even Mother Nature revealed her dismay as the sky brought forth a warm, gentle rain. Tears of sadness fell from the heavens while all the land mourned the loss of a true and mighty friend. Fée from every corner of Calabiyau came to the castle to pay homage, leaving thousands of flowers of every color and type along the abundant courtyard walkways. Their rich fragrances filled the air with royal splendor. Deer, squirrels, skunks, bears, birds, and raccoons also paused to say good-bye as Fée and creatures joined together for one last tribute to their beloved king.

It was the beginning of a new cycle, and with it, a new leader. Like the changing of the seasons, one had relinquished its claim, and another was about to take its place. King Toeyad was gone and Kandide, now possessed of the Gift, was to be crowned.

The High Council, Calabiyau's governing body, was to perform Kandide's official crowning on the fourth sunrise. Normally, the Fée would set aside seven days in reverence to a king's passing, and then another week before the crowning. King Toeyad, however, as his last official order to the Council, had forbidden it. He made the twelve Council members promise to have no reverence at all and to crown Kandide on the fourth day after she received the Gift.

Toeyad argued that four days was plenty of time to make the necessary preparations. "I have lived in happiness," he told them. "I shall pass leaving nothing less. Crown my daughter quickly, rejoice in your new queen, and let the cycle begin anew. I fear there are dangers yet untold and Calabiyau must not appear vulnerable to Banshee or Fée. Do this as I request, and I shall rest as I have lived, in peace and harmony."

To the lack of official reverence, as well as Kandide's immediate crowning, the Council members had no choice but to abide. It was, after all, the law of the land that the passing king shall have the final say in these matters.

And while, like most of the High Council, many of her subjects did not like Kandide's arrogant ways, it was also true that few of them had actually met her. Rumors, however, did abound of her selfish, spoiled nature. "Surely, Kandide has inherited some of her father's better traits and is not as intolerable as they say," many of her subjects would optimistically propose. "After all, she is of her father's essence." Others would vehemently disagree, stating that they personally knew of someone who had felt the wrath of her arrogant ways and self-centered whims.

Nevertheless, Kandide was to be their queen. Arrogant or not, it was her destiny. That was the law of the land.

Kandide always had her father for support.
Now that support was gone.

TWELVE

O ver the next couple of days, Kandide became even more radiant. How incredibly lovely she looked with the Gift of the Frost now glowing so strongly within her. Even her wings looked as though they had captured the multifaceted prism of a rainbow. Never had she been more beautiful—or more stoically dispassionate to those around her.

After all, she rationalized, *was it not Father who taught me that I must be strong and never reveal my emotions? Was it not he who forbade any reverence? And was it not he who insisted that I be crowned in just four days?*

Kandide always had her father for support. Now that support was gone. And if the truth was really to be known, she missed him terribly and was extremely upset by his passing, even a little frightened. That truth, however, must never be known. Kandide would not even admit it to herself.

"Father would be so very proud of how beautiful I look today," she remarked to Teren as they ventured out to the gaming fields. "I do so wish he were here . . . to see how radiant I am, I mean." Her excessive vanity seemed to be her way of compensating for the tremendous loneliness she dared not express. "Don't you just love the way my wings glow? You know, Teren, since Father's passing, no one has seen me shed a tear."

"Yeah, yeah, yeah!" As usual, he was completely unimpressed with his sister's carrying on, especially so close to their father's passing. "I'm sure Father would be really proud of the way you are . . . I mean, your wings are glowing," he added with a strong note of sarcasm. "Now come on, let's go."

On this bright sunny day, he and Kandide were headed off for an early morning bout of aerial cane fighting, or aercaen, as the Fée call it. Requiring far more strategy and speed than physical strength, aercaen was one of the more challenging of the faery battle games. It was also one of Kandide's absolute favorites. She had won many a match because of her considerable skill and wit in out-maneuvering her opponents.

Kandide was dressed entirely in white. And while her attire was perfectly designed for playing aercaen, typical of the future queen, it was far more ornate than necessary. Teren, on the other hand, was dressed in the traditional dark-blue practice uniform.

"It's such a shame that I have to deploy the Gift to change the seasons." She was twirling her fighting stick between her fingers. "I mean, I just hate the fact that when I do, my wonderful glow will go away."

"Yeah, well, it's more of a shame that I let you talk me into coming out here. Besides," Teren halfheartedly cajoled, "your 'wonderful glow' will build back up way before you have to deploy the Gift again next year."

Wishing that he had not agreed to play, Teren was anxious to get the game over. Given his preference, he would have stayed in the Royal Library, hiding out among the shelves of ancient books. Since almost no one ever went up there, it was the only place he felt secure enough to express his overwhelming grief.

Ignoring her brother's comments, Kandide exclaimed, "That's it!"

"That's what?"

"After my crowning parties, then I shall bring about the Frost. I shall order the parties to continue for days. That way, with the radiance of the Gift, all of my subjects will see how incredibly beautiful I am."

"They already know how beautiful you are."

"Well, of course they do, Teren, but now—"

"But now, big sister, I think they'd rather see how beautiful the frost looks. It's really late for the seasons to change, you know—way past Samhain."

"Yes, but look at all the lovely weather I am allowing." She gestured toward the bright blue sky. The air was fresh, and the morning sky was, indeed, clear, with only a few wispy clouds scattered about. The temperature was ideal for being on the gaming field.

"I've made up my mind," Kandide declared, while flitting about and practicing maneuvers with her cane, "deploying the Frost will have to wait until I am ready. After all, delaying winter for a few more days will give me . . . I mean, my subjects more time to spend in the meadows."

"Okay! Okay! Can we just play now?" Teren was completely fed up with Kandide's unrelenting, self-absorbed attitude. He would not have even consented to play with her, except for her badgering and the fact that he had yet to beat her in a single match—a fact that, on this day, he hoped to change. Unbeknownst to his sister, the young prince had a brand new trick up his sleeve. Although Toeyad made him promise not to use it until he had practiced, his father said nothing about whom he should practice it on.

Teren shouted the signal to start the match. "Cotell!"

They both lowered their protective face guards and the game began. Soaring above the field, their hard wooden sticks began clashing as they tumbled and whirled through the air. Kandide was, as always, the epitome of poise. Even in battle games, her graceful carriage never seemed to falter. And while Teren was a bit clumsier, she couldn't help but notice how much he had improved since last they competed. She even felt a touch of pride in the fact that her little brother might actually be taking something other than his books on spellmaking seriously. Ducking and dodging, the two siblings swung and hit at each other as though their very lives depended on the outcome.

Observing a properly played game of aercaen is like watching an aerial ballet that has been choreographed for brutal combat. The object of the game is to either maneuver the opponent to the ground, or cause the opponent to drop his or her cane— the only weapon players are allowed to use. Since air offers no resistance, often it is clever tactics, quick thinking, and balance, more than sheer force, that determines the winner. Other than not actually killing one's opponent, there are no real rules. Combatants simply keep playing five-minute rounds until one or the other, due to lack of skill or exhaustion, is defeated.

With a carefully executed flip, Kandide was just about to smash the cane from her brother's hand, when she quite literally froze in midair.

"In honor of Father, we shall go to the meadows and bring back some pomegranates for my crowning parties."

THIRTEEN

"I t works!" Teren hollered. "It works!" Seizing the advantage, he easily knocked the cane from a very frozen Kandide's hands. "It really works!" he repeated, astonished by the results of his new spell. "Father said it would!"

Suddenly waking up, Kandide shook her head, not at all aware of what her brother had done. "What . . . was that? What happened? What did—"

"I . . . uh . . . beat you!" Teren proudly responded as he floated to the ground.

"No, you cheated, that's what you did!" Still a bit dazed, Kandide nonetheless managed a graceful landing. "You put a spell on me, and that, little brother, is not allowed!"

"Where does it say so in the rules?"

"Well, it certainly isn't proper gaming etiquette." Noticing Tiyana and her sister standing to one side of the field, Kandide continued, "Is it, Mother?"

"I'm not quite sure," Tiyana chuckled. Attempting to keep a straight face, she and Tara approached the two of them. "I don't think it has ever been an issue before."

"Well, it is an issue now! And I am quite sure that I will not play with you again, little brother, if you must resort to using your silly spells to win!" Shoving her face mask at him, Kandide turned to leave.

"You're just jealous 'cause you can't do this spell!"

"All right, Teren, that is enough," Tiyana reprimanded.

"Oh, now it's my fault. It's always my fault!" With his arms crossed and his feet firmly planted on the ground, he glared at his older sister.

Not able to resist, Kandide spun around to face her brother. Mimicking his posture, she retorted, "It usually is!"

"That is not what I meant, Kandide, and you know it." Tiyana spoke to her daughter in the same firm tone. "Now, I need you back at the castle. There is a great deal to be done for your crowning ceremonies tomorrow, not to mention the parties afterward."

"Better run along, Kandide!" Teren chided, quickly turning his attention to Tara. "Hey, Tara, want to see how my new spell works?"

"Sure, I'd love t—"

"She can't!" Kandide hastily cut her sister off. "We are going to the meadows, aren't we, Tara?"

"Well . . . I . . . uh . . ."

Ignoring Tara's hesitation, Kandide was insistent. "That is what we shall do. In honor of Father, we shall go to the meadows and bring back some pomegranates for my crowning parties."

"I absolutely forbid it!" Tiyana exclaimed. "I'm told there may be a storm coming. And you have much too much to do to ready yourself for the ceremonies."

"Oh, Mother, you never like me to go to the meadows. I want one last bit of freedom before I become a captive to my crown!" Kandide was almost belligerent in her insistence.

How she loved the meadows, even more than the games. To her, they were a place of such beauty and tranquility. As a child, she and her father would sneak away from his courtly duties to go there and pick pomegranates. The picking usually turned into a lively game of catch. Then, exhausted, the two of them would break open the ripest, stuffing themselves with the jewel-like ruby fruit as they relaxed on thick moss under a shady tree.

"Kandide, please do not go there today," her mother implored.

"But I want to. Are you coming, Tara?"

Tara looked at her mother to see what she should do. "I . . . ah . . . ?"

"Go ahead, Tara. If Kandide must go, then maybe you can ensure that she doesn't stay too long." Tiyana knew that this battle was one she probably would not win. And even if she did, Kandide would spend the rest of the day pouting instead of getting anything done.

"I'll help you, Mother," Teren offered in his most endearing fashion.

"Thank you, Teren. There are, however, still some decisions that only Kandide can make."

"Then I shall make them when I return. Let's be off, little sister."

Tara started to gesture so that the two of them might magically transport to the meadows. Kandide, however, had already decided that they would take advantage of the warm weather by flying all the way there, just as she and their father had done so many times before. She grabbed her sister's hand, insisting, "No, I want to fly." Pulling Tara off the ground, up they sailed.

"Teren, don't you dare!" Tiyana ordered, seeing that her son was about to "practice" his new spell again.

"Ahh . . . you never let me have any fun!"

"Come along! There are a few things you can help me with, and that is not one of them." With a magical phrase and wave of her hands, Tiyana gestured to transport the two of them back to the castle. Instantly, they vanished, dissolving into a shimmering spray of faery dust.

FOURTEEN

Across the castle grounds, over three separate villages, and out into the open spaces the two sisters flew. Below, they could see thousands of Fée still leaving flowers for their father—*and my crowning, of course,* Kandide thought. "Tomorrow I will deal with all of that," she commented to Tara, "but right now I am free. We have the entire day to enjoy the meadows."

Together, they flew between the treetops, across the streams, and down into the valley. It was a beautiful day—perfect for catching sunbeams. The sisters laughed and giggled, playing with butterflies and songbirds along the way. Before long, they reached the meadows, which were very beautiful that time of the year, very peaceful, and so very full of wild pomegranate trees. The vibrant green grass stretched on like a vast emerald carpet, and since the first frost had not yet fallen, hundreds of late-blooming flowers still dotted the terrain. Purple and yellow, red and gold, the blossoms glistened in the sun with the last drops of morning dew. Their fragrance made the air smell fresh and sweet.

Fluttering up to the top of a tree, Kandide plucked a luscious pomegranate. Laughing, she tossed it to Tara and a game of aerial catch ensued. The hours passed as they darted from tree to tree, selecting the largest of the fruit for their own and tossing the smaller ones to the animals waiting below. Foxes, raccoons, and white-striped skunks all joined in the feasting. They squealed and snorted with joy each time a fruit was discarded. A large buck tossed his head, braying in appreciation. He also loved the freshly picked fruit, sweet from the sunlight that reached the top of the trees.

Suddenly, Tara realized that the sun had begun to dim. The air felt heavy, and the sky was getting darker and darker by the moment. Thunderclouds were rolling in, and she knew, all too well, that the meadows were no place to be in a storm. With the sudden wind whirling around her, and large drops of rain starting to fall, the weather was beginning to look as though it could get ugly. Even the animals were rushing to take shelter.

"We'd better go," Tara called out.

"In a minute, Tara. I want to gather a few more pomegranates from up here. Don't worry, we'll be fine." Kandide gleefully tossed her sister a large red fruit. "See how perfect these are."

But before Tara could catch the pomegranate, a blinding flash of lightning streaked down from the sky. Her heart nearly stopped. Over the piercing clap of thunder, she heard her sister's terrified scream.

Panicked, Tara gasped, "No! Nooo! It can't be!"

But it was.

Branches came crashing down, and, with them, a very limp Kandide plummeted to the moss below.

"Kandi!" Tara screamed, rushing to her sister's side. Already, the silver radiance that surrounded her was beginning to fade. Propping Kandide's head up, Tara could see the dimming semblance of its glow. "Kandi, wake up! Wake up!" she cried. "Please, Kandi, please, wake up!"

Her words, however, were to no avail. Kandide's injuries were severe. Tara instantly realized that her own healing skills, as powerful as they were, would not be nearly enough to save her sister's life. It would require the help of several healers, and even then, she was petrified that Kandide might die. Tara knew that she had only minutes to get her sister back to the castle. But first, she needed to transfer at least some energy into Kandide. Transferring too much would mean that Tara would be left without the strength to get them both home; not enough, and her sister's essence would continue to fade.

With thunder crashing overhead, and the rain beginning to pour, Tara mustered all of her strength. As she placed her hands on Kandide's temples to channel precious life back into her, she could feel her sister improve only slightly. Kandide's life source was almost completely knocked out by the lightning strike. Had it not been for the extra energy from inheriting the Gift, she surely would not have survived even this long. Tara knew that getting her home quickly, where multiple healers could link their energies together, was crucial.

But how?

She knew better than to attempt to fly home. If lightning should strike them while in the sky, it would be fatal to them both. Transporting her sister back to the castle was almost as dangerous, but with Kandide so weak, it might be her only hope.

Timing was crucial. If Tara should happen to time the transport wrong, their essence could be sucked into the electrical surge caused by the lightning. *We must transport during a momentary break in the flashes,* she thought, looking up at the ominous dark clouds.

Terrified and soaked from the pouring rain, Tara pulled Kandide tightly against her own body. As soon as she saw a streak of lightning flash across the sky, she instantly gestured to transport, hoping beyond hope that another would not occur for a few minutes. *May the earthly spirits be with us,* she thought, as the two of them faded into nothingness.

Even in their transported state, Tara could hear thunder booming around her. Brilliant flashes began erupting in the distance, one right after another. Hopefully, luck would be on their side and they were far enough away from the deadly strikes. Hopefully, she had guessed right on the timing.

FIFTEEN

Inside the castle, Tiyana heard the thunder and was frantic. Memories of her twin sister lost from just such a storm began filling her thoughts. "I do hope they get back soon, Teren," she sighed, pacing back and forth, as she looked outside at the dark sky and torrential rain.

"I can go look for them," he suggested.

"No, you know it is far too dangerous." Tiyana watched yet another fiery bolt of lightning strike. A second later, she heard its deep rumbling thunder. "That was much too close."

"Mother!" Appearing on the landing atop the grand stairway, Tara screamed for help. "Mother!" She clung to Kandide who was, by now, extremely pale. Both were dripping wet.

"May the spirits help us!" Tiyana shrieked as she saw her two daughters. "Teren, gather as many of the healers as you can find, then send them upstairs, immediately!"

Tiyana instantly rushed up to the landing. She helped Tara carry Kandide to her chamber, where they removed her soaked clothing and gently placed her into bed. With virtually all of her essence drained, Kandide was unconscious and growing evermore translucent. Both Tiyana and Tara knew it was a sign that she would not last much longer. Lightning is one of the Fée's worst natural enemies. Even the Fire clan respects its power and would never dare to venture out in such a storm.

Servants, then the healers began flooding Kandide's chamber. Creating a linked circle with the others, an exhausted Tara started channeling their combined energies directly into Kandide. In Fée terms, what her sister needed was almost a total energy transfusion. Even then, she might not survive.

For the next two days, Kandide lay motionless, barely clinging to life. Although completely exhausted, neither Tara, Teren, nor Tiyana would leave her side. Each time Tara renewed a little of her own strength, she and the other healers immediately channeled more energy into Kandide.

But there was no response, no movement, no sign from Kandide that she would survive. Their only faint hope was that she was slowly becoming less translucent.

SIXTEEN

Inside the chamber of the High Council—a large mahogany paneled room that seemed almost too austere in its décor—every conversation revolved around the future queen. The Council of Twelve, as the members were commonly called, represented the twelve primary Fée clans—Earth, Water, Fire, Plants, Science, Air, Animals, History, Creativity, Wisdom, Healing Arts, and the Heart. Each of these twelve clans has its own subset of clans who are the guardians of the weather, ice and snow, music, the forest, wizardry, spells, the oceans and seas, rocks and gems, flowers, insects, knowledge, medicine, the crops, and hundreds more. Not a single aspect of faery life is without its keepers.

Collectively, the Council members were quite powerful and often extremely vocal when it came to deciding matters of state, especially as they related to Princess Kandide.

"If only Kandide had not gone to the meadows," sighed Lady Alicia, one of the Council members. She was a guardian of reptiles, and her clan was that of the Animals. Lady Alicia had been a member of the High Council since its inception, nearly one hundred years prior.

"Unfortunately, Lady Alicia," replied Lord Socrat, whose clan members were among the wisest of the Fée, "*if* might be Kandide's favorite conjunction, but it cannot help her, or us, right now." He and his wife, Lady Socrat, who was of the Forest guardians and represented the Plants clan, also had been Council members since its beginning.

"You are absolutely right, Lord Socrat," interjected a Council member named Lady Corale. Her clan was of the Water, and she was a guardian of the oceans and seas. "It certainly will not alter the unfortunate situation that Kandide has placed upon us."

Lady Karena, whose clan was of the Heart, was always the most tolerant of Kandide. "You mustn't be so critical, Lady Corale. Surely she will recover, and all will be w—"

Before Lady Karena could finish her sentence, an intensely bright scarlet flash of light erupted near the Council chamber entrance. Materializing in all her blazing splendor was Lady Aron of the Fire clan. "Perhaps, Lady Karena," the fiery Fée quipped most acerbically, "we will all be blessed and Kandide will not recov—I mean . . . pass."

Dressed in vibrant reds, scarlets, yellows, and ambers, with hair and wings that shimmered as though they were forged of flames, Lady Aron was anything but a fan of Kandide's. The stubborn, self-absorbed nature of both seemed to put them on

LADY ARON

a constant collision course. Kandide's recent behavior and the desperate situation that they were now facing added even more fuel to Lady Aron's perpetually hot temper. Each time she spoke of the future queen, her amber eyes with their piercing blue pupils flashed in unbridled annoyance. "I don't mean to imply that this untimely accident was poetic justice or anything, but we all know that Kandide has never shown respect. Had she attended to her duties instead of going to the meadows, none of this would have occurred. I am quite sure we can all agree that this time her actions set a new standard for reproach."

"Speaking of reproach, must you always enter like that?" Lady Batony glared at her. She was from the Creativity clan and a guardian of music. "It's most annoying. Besides, it is the Gift of the Frost that we must be concerned with now."

"Surprisingly enough, Lady Batony, I agree with you—about the Gift, that is." Lady Aron nonchalantly walked over to assume her place at one end of the large crescent-shaped Council table. Seated next to her husband, Lord Aron, she continued speaking in her usual indifferent manner. "My apologies to all of you for being late. I was attending to other duties."

Ignoring her apology, Lady Batony continued, "The real question is, what if Kandide does not recover? What of the Gift?"

"We must at least consider that possibility," Lord Revên, of the Science clan, replied. "This is a very serious situation."

"That it is," Lord Aron concurred, nodding his head. "And from what I have been told, there is a possibility that she may, indeed, not recover." Soft-spoken, he was from the Earth clan and a most handsome Fée. With chocolate-brown hair and dark-brown eyes, Lord Aron was the complete antithesis of his fiery wife. "We all know that the Gift must be—"

"Preserved at any cost," Lady Aron interrupted, something she did quite frequently.

"Speaking of which," Lady Batony retorted, "are you suggesting that—"

"I'm not suggesting anything."

"All right. All right," Lord Rössi cut her off. "You two . . . please." Lord Rössi, whose clan members were the Historians and the keepers of the records for all time, was the Council chair. "Must you bicker even at a time such as this? You are certainly not helping the situation—either of you!"

"I am told by my healers that Kandide has some color returning," Lord Salitar hastily interjected. His clan members were the guardians of the Healing Arts.

"We can only hope you are right," Lord Standish sighed. His clan was of the Air. At nearly four hundred fifty years old, he was the eldest member of the Council.

While many of the Council members were quick to express their concerns, none of them seemed to have any idea what to do about the injured crown princess, and more importantly, the Gift.

After a great deal of discussion, Lady Aron finally suggested, "Kandide has been a problem since she was born. If what you say is true, Lord Salitar, then as soon as she gains any semblance of consciousness, she must be ordered to transfer the Gift to someone who can immediately deploy it."

"Someone like you, Lady Aron?" Here, too, Lady Batony did not miss the chance to throw a barb at the Fire Fée.

Before she could answer, Lady Karena protested, "But transferring the Gift could kill Kandide in her weakened state."

Smiling, Lady Aron shrugged, "And so it might. Again, I ask, do any of you have a better solution?" The thought of actually ridding Calabiyau of Kandide's presence was far too exhilarating for Lady Aron to control her glee.

Almost from the time Kandide could speak, King Toeyad had taken the crown princess to the High Council sessions. And, even when she was a child, he would ask her opinion on important matters of state. He always encouraged her to speak up—something Kandide never had any trouble doing. Then, to the utter dismay of the Council—especially Lady Aron— Toeyad actually considered her suggestions as seriously as he did those of its members.

When criticized for it, as he continually was, he would simply smile and say, "My daughter must learn to assess all matters, for one day her decisions will have the power to challenge the fates."

In spite of the Council members' overheated debating, Lady Aron ultimately convinced them to agree on one thing: "Above all else, the Gift must be preserved, regardless of the cost. All life depends upon it."

"What's . . . what's wrong? Mother?
What's wrong with everyone?"

SEVENTEEN

On the third day following the accident, Teren thought he noticed his sister stir. Albeit ever so slightly, Kandide had, indeed, moved her head. "Mother! Mother, come here. I think she . . . she's waking up!"

"Thank the earthly spirits!" Rushing over to Kandide's bedside, Tiyana knelt down beside her daughter. "The channeling may have been enough. Kandide . . . Kandide, can you hear me?"

Slowly, Kandide's eyes fluttered open. Although still very groggy, she managed to whisper, "Mo . . . Mother . . . ? What . . . what hap—?" As Kandide struggled to sit up, relief sprang forth from the rest of the assemblage of healers who quickly gathered around her bed.

"Hush now, my child." Tiyana gently stroked her daughter's forehead, brushing a golden wisp of hair away from her eyes. "Be still. You are very weak. You were struck by lightning. Tara brought you home."

Kandide's eyes began to focus, and a faint smile crossed her lips. "Tara . . . I . . . I . . ."

"It's okay." The elated young princess reached down to hold her sister's hand. "You're going to be all right now, Kandi. That's all that matters."

Incredibly, as soon as Tara touched her, a sudden surge of energy flowed throughout Kandide's body. The radiant glow of the Gift began to reappear, once again surrounding her with a silvery halo. Kandide's color and strength instantly returned. "Mother, look! I'm okay." She held out her hands, turning them from back to front for all to see the glow. "I am okay."

Kandide was alive, but all was not okay. For as she leaned forward, her left wing did not unfold. The healers' expressions quickly changed from joy to shock. Daring not to speak, they simply stood there with mouths open, staring at their future queen.

"What . . . what's wrong? Mother? What's wrong with everyone?" Looking back at her wing, Kandide shrieked. "No! It can't be! My wing! My beautiful wing! It's . . . it's . . . bent!"

Kandide's left wing was no longer full and beautiful. Instead of silver and gossamer, it looked like crumpled parchment— dull, twisted, and grotesquely deformed. She was barely able to move it. When she tried, agonizing pains shot up and down her back and shoulders.

As the realization of her plight began to sink in, Kandide became frantic, demanding of Tara and the other healers, "You must fix it! I command all of you to fix my wing. Now!"

One by one, the healers lowered their heads, not wishing to meet Kandide's flashing eyes.

"Why don't you answer me? How could you have let this happen?" Kandide began shouting. "You must fix it! I can't be . . . Not me! I won't be a . . . I won't be an Imperfect. A . . . a crumplewing! Even for a minute!"

"Kandide, please, calm down," Tiyana urged. "It will take time, and you need to rest."

"No, I want them to fix it right now." Her father's words of strength and courage reverberated within her head. Attempting to gain some semblance of composure, she resolutely demanded, "You must heal my wing, now! As your queen, I command it!"

"Of course, they will try," Tiyana responded, hoping to lessen her daughter's fury.

"I don't want them to try, Mother. I want them to fix it. Right now!" Kandide glared at her mother, then at the others, and finally at her sister. "Tell me you can do it, Tara! Tell me you can fix it!"

"We'll do our best, Kandi." From experience, however, Tara knew that, unless Kandide's wing had been repaired immediately after it was damaged, there was very little hope of it ever being perfect again. Kandide was so weak when she brought her back to the castle that all of their channeling went into just keeping her alive.

Lars, one of the senior healers, spoke up, "Your wing was severely damaged, Your Majesty. Even if Tara were at her full strength, I don't think it is within our powers—at least not immediately. Perhaps over time . . ." The others nodded in agreement.

Realizing that his words might possibly be true, Kandide became even more enraged. With nowhere else to vent, she shouted at Tara, "This is your fault! You've always been jealous of me!"

"But, Kandi, I—" Shocked at the accusation, Tara desperately tried to make her sister understand. "We've done everythi—"

"You've done nothing. You're jealous of my beauty—that's what it is!" Breathing heavily, Kandide's shrill response continued, "Now go! Everyone go! You, too, Mother!" Turning away, she sank back into her bed. As if to deny the truth, she covered her head with the bed's thick blue satin comforter.

Tiyana desperately tried to comfort her daughter, but alas, Kandide refused her attempts. Instead, she simply screamed from under the covers for her mother to go away. There was nothing Tiyana could do. Perhaps nothing anyone could do. Her beautiful and oh-so-perfect daughter, the soon-to-be queen, was now a crumplewing—an Imperfect. To the Fée, and more importantly, to Kandide, it was a fate of unimaginable horror.

Since the beginning of time, Imperfects, as the Fée called those who were not physically perfect, were considered to be a disgrace. They were simply not accepted and sent away. While there was growing sympathy towards the plight of Imperfects, no one had the power to override the majority.

Although rarely discussed in polite society, it was assumed that, once Imperfects were banished, most did not survive for very long. A small number ventured into the realm of human-kind—an easy task for the Fée, since, unlike humans, they can travel from one dimension to another. However, since fullblooded faeries age very quickly in the human dimension, they cannot remain there for very long. Even the Fée who do visit are usually destined to be alone, since all but the most perceptive simply deny their existence.

Before leaving Kandide's room, Tiyana placed a mild sleeping spell on her daughter. It was to calm her, as much as to ease her pain. She and the others then reluctantly left the crown princess.

"Mylea, please stay near," Tiyana requested of Kandide's lady-in-waiting as she departed her daughter's antechamber. "Call me as soon as she wakes."

Mylea nodded. "Yes, Your Majesty. I will, of course."

"I'm so sorry, Mother," Tara exclaimed. Exhausted, she was nearly in tears. "I would never do anything to hurt Kandi . . . never."

"Of course you wouldn't. You saved her life, child." Tiyana put her arm around her youngest daughter. "It is not your fault, Tara. You must not feel like it is. No one could have done more to help Kandide than you. No one."

"Maybe I could use some magic to create a glamour spell," Teren eagerly suggested, not knowing what else to say.

"I'm afraid it would take an extraordinary amount of magic and glamour to conceal that much damage," Tiyana sighed. "And even then, the spell could not be sustained for very long—not even by your wizardry, my son. No, we must inform the Council."

As Tiyana and her two children walked down the long corridor that led to the Council chamber, she could only think of one thing: the continual battle that Lady Aron waged against Imperfects.

"Physical perfection is imperative to the survival of the Fée," Lady Aron would repeat, time and time again. "Imperfects are weak and an embarrassment. They are a threat to all we have stood for since the beginning of time. They must never be allowed to remain in our land, or before you know it, they will expect to live among us. Our governing Articles have never accepted them for that reason. That is the way it has always been, and that is the way it will remain, as long as I serve on the Council."

Since the vote of the Council needed to be unanimous in order to amend the Articles, King Toeyad had little choice but to concede to Lady Aron's demands. Even after nearly a hundred years of trying, the most he could evoke was the tolerance to allow those Fée with minor imperfections to conceal their flaws. Life, however, was very difficult for those who used glamour to do so. They were relegated to the most menial of tasks and were certainly not allowed to live among the higher levels of Fée society. The idea of an Imperfect becoming queen was unfathomable, something Tiyana knew all too well.

"Do we have to tell the Council what happened to Kandide's wing right now, Mother?" Teren queried, just before he, Tara, and Tiyana were to enter their chamber.

"Unfortunately, we do, Teren—they must be told the truth." This would not be easy for Tiyana, but do it she must. "Better I tell them now than they hear it from someone else. We shall deal with the consequences later."

EIGHTEEN

Each of the twelve members of the Council bowed to acknowledge Tiyana and the two siblings. The dark mahogany wood that paneled the Council Chamber seemed somehow ironically appropriate at that moment. And, although the mood was somber, all were anxious to hear what she had to say.

"What is the news?" a very concerned Lord Socrat inquired. He and Lady Socrat were Tiyana's oldest and most trusted friends.

"My daughter lives," Tiyana replied.

Sighs of relief spread throughout. A gesture of Tiyana's hand, however, indicated that there was more to tell. "She lives, however . . ."

"However what, Tiyana?" demanded Lady Aron, whose words, like her beauty, contained no semblance of softness.

Lady Aron was the most belligerent and argumentative Fée Tiyana had ever known, and was, perhaps, the only Council member she truly did not like or trust.

"Kandide is injured."

"Injured? In what way, Tiyana?" Lord Rössi inquired. His tone was far more sympathetic.

"She . . . She has an injured wi—"

"Tell them, Mother. Tell them how the healers have failed me!" Dropping her cloak, Kandide revealed the awful truth; one wing was terribly bent and broken.

Shock spread among the Council members. "No!" "This cannot be!" "No, it . . . Kandide!"

All she could hear were shrieks of disbelief combined with gasps of horror. Momentary confusion reigned as the Council members began muttering among themselves. Most of them had never seen a wing so badly damaged. While they might have felt pity for Kandide, many could not help but also feel a sense of repulsion. She was, after all, an Imperfect. And of all the imperfections, having a crumpled wing was considered one of the worst, since perfect wings are a point of pride to the Fée.

As was usually the case, Lady Aron, with calculated indifference, spoke up. There was almost a sense of delight in her voice. "Well, then, as I see it, the solution is really quite simple. Kandide must be sent away, and Tara will immediately be crowned queen."

"Me?" Tara gasped. "No, no, no, no . . . NO! I cannot be queen."

"What of the Gift?" Lady Batony quickly interjected.

Lady Aron glared straight at Kandide. "Yes, the Gift. Since I doubt that you have the strength to deploy it, it must be instantly transferred to someone else."

"Yes, transferred." "Today!" "We mustn't wait!" One voice overlapped another as the Council members each added his or her sentiments to the ensuing disorder.

"It must happen now!"

"Yes, now!"

"Silence! Please," Tiyana demanded, completely appalled by the Council's behavior. "My daughter has nearly passed and all you can think of is transferring the Gift! She is not strong enough to do so right now. It would surely kill her."

Regardless of how cruel she sounded, Lady Aron never missed a chance to wield her authority, especially when it came to Kandide. This, however, was a moment that even she could not have dared to hope for. "Your daughter is an Imperfect, Tiyana, a crumplewing." Truly relishing the moment, the fiery Fée's words became even more biting: "Kandide, you no longer belong among us. First you get yourself injured through your self-centered actions, and then you disgrace and humiliate your entire family by coming in here and displaying your hideous deformity. Your behavior is a grave dishonor to your father and to this crown. I demand that you transfer the Gift of the Frost—and that you do it immediately!"

"How dare you demand anything of me, the rightful heir to his throne!" Kandide's response was equally as forceful. "Let me remind you, Lady Aron, that you have no authority to insist that I do anything. I shall speak to my subjects, and then we shall see about the Gift, and my future!"

"Well, I do hope that you will show your dear family at least some respect and leave Calabiyau as soon as you are able," retorted an even more incensed Lady Aron. "At least until your wing can be healed—if that is even possible!" Her golden eyes were blazing. "May I remind you that the Frost is already severely overdue? You must either immediately deploy the Gift, or transfer it to someone who is strong enough to do so."

Kandide glared back at her. "Perhaps, but that will be my decision." Pulling her cape back up around her shoulders, she grandly swept out of the chamber. Crumplewing or not, she was the rightful queen, and no one, least of all Lady Aron, would tell her what to do, or when to do it!

Under her breath, Lady Aron sneered, "We'll see."

NINETEEN

I n the courtyard, thousands of Fée from every clan had gathered below the castle's main balcony. The afternoon was bright and sunny and all were awaiting news of their new queen. As Kandide walked out onto the large platform where her father had spoken to his subjects so many times before, the sound of long-horned trumpets heralded her arrival.

Followed closely by Tiyana, Tara, and Teren, Kandide stepped forward, raising her hand to greet her subjects. Upon seeing her, the anxious crowd began wildly cheering. Cries of, "She lives!" and "Long live Queen Kandide!" began erupting, followed by applause and more cheering.

Kandide raised her hand again, this time to silence the overflowing crowd. "Yes, I live." She ceremoniously nodded and more cheers poured forth. Smiling, Kandide continued, "You are my loyal subjects, and I am soon to be crowned your queen. It is my destiny to serve in the footsteps of my father, our greatest and most beloved King Toeyad."

Again cheers erupted, and again she silenced them with yet another wave of her hand. "Hear me now; I must take leave for a brief while so that I may fully regain my strength and return to take my father's place as your beloved monarch."

"No!"

"Why?"

"What's wrong?"

She could hear their questioning as uncertainty spread throughout the assemblage.

"Do not fear; I shall not be gone for long. It was with strength and courage that King Toeyad led you, and it was only through my own strength and courage that I survived the lightning. And survive I did. It is my destiny to be your greatest ruler, and that I shall be."

The crowd went silent again. This time, however, it was a result of her extreme arrogance, not her gesturing.

"My sister, Princess Tara, will reign in my brief absence." With a deep, formal curtsy, Kandide acknowledged her sister as the temporary queen. As she rose, however, one of the trumpeters who turned to aid her stepped on her cape, causing it to pull away from her shoulders.

There, for all to see, was her terrible secret.

Appalled and shocked, dissension began rippling through the crowd. "She's a crumplewing!" someone shouted. Jeers and laughter followed as awareness of her imperfection spread. Taunting cries began resonating throughout the courtyard. "Kandide's a crumplewing!" "Kandi Crumplewing, Kandi

Crumplewing, you're no queen!" The chant became louder and louder, until suddenly a pomegranate pelted her in the shoulder, knocking her backwards. Then another hit her, and another narrowly missed. The crowd was spiraling out of control.

Fearing for her daughter's life, Tiyana frantically gestured. With a wave of her hand, Kandide disappeared; only her shimmering essence remained. Stunned silence befell the assemblage below as they watched their once-future queen vanish into nothingness.

"Princess Kandide has been sent away," pronounced Tiyana, who, for a brief moment, scanned the faces in the crowd. She then abruptly turned and, without another word, left the balcony. With every ounce of strength that she could muster, Tiyana walked down the long hall and back into the Council chamber. "Kandide has been sent away," she reiterated to the Council.

"What?" Lady Aron demanded. "The Gift! What about the Gift?"

Tiyana looked scornfully at her, then at each of the twelve members, replying, "The Gift? The present is the Gift that you should consider now, for it will determine how we unwrap our future. I suggest you consider it and your actions here today most wisely."

Tiyana turned and, saying nothing more, left the Council chamber. First her beloved King Toeyad, and then Kandide. This was surely a time that would require a great deal of strength and courage. But done was done. The fates had staked their claim. Tara and Teren need her now, and she must determine how to unwrap their future wisely. Tara was in no way prepared to be queen. It would be an interesting journey.

She could only hope that Kandide would also find her way.

TWENTY

Kandide hadn't intended to fall asleep, only to rest until daybreak. Emerging from the last few remnants of slumber, it took her a few minutes to remember what had happened—that her mother had sent her away, and that she had taken refuge in this small cave just before nightfall.

Maybe I'm dreaming, she thought. The severe pain in her shoulder, however, told her otherwise. As the confused princess lay there attempting to make sense of it all, she felt something cold and wet nudging her arm. Slowly turning to look, Kandide saw a huge silver-gray wolf looming over her. It was the biggest wolf she had ever seen.

Inching herself away from the creature, she managed to stammer, "H . . . Hello. I . . . I won't hurt you." She held out her hand for him to sniff, but the wolf merely glared at her, his amber eyes glowing in the dim light of the cave. "Rea . . . really

I won't. Nice boy." For what seemed like an eternity, but was, indeed, only a few seconds, he stood there watching her. Then, with a deep-throated growl, he turned and ambled out of the cave. Pausing for a moment to look back at her, the animal then disappeared into the tangled woods.

I need to get out of here. Hastily standing up, Kandide straightened her dress, pulled the cape around her shoulders, and cautiously stepped outside. Her crumpled wing was throbbing, but that was something she would just have to endure for the time being. Looking in each direction, she had no idea which way to go. She only knew that she must find a way out of this terrible place, and quickly.

Although the sun had risen, the forest was still engulfed in the same strange dark fog. Any light that shone through cast ominous shadows, making the gnarled dead forest appear even more menacing than when she had first arrived. Taking a few steps in one direction, Kandide spotted the wolf standing only a dozen meters away. He was partially hidden behind a massive old fallen oak. His amber eyes were watching her every move. Again he growled.

Maybe not that way, she thought, quickly turning in the opposite direction. Being extra careful not to slip, Kandide slowly began making her way through the tangled tree branches and marshy underbrush. The wolf had left her alone once; she did not want to press her luck by moving too fast and possibly falling, or by appearing to be even the slightest bit afraid. She knew all too well that beasts of prey can sense fear. Even though wolves rarely attack Fée, now was neither the time nor the place to tempt fate.

As Kandide reached out to snap a twisted branch that blocked her way, she had a sudden thought. *Maybe these are the Mists? Maybe this is where Imperfects are sent. Maybe that is the reason no one ever sees them again.* She remembered back to the time when she believed that sending Imperfects to a place like this was merely a legend—a ruse to make young Fée behave. A wave of panic swept over her. *Maybe it is true.*

"No. No! I will not think about that! I must keep focused." Repeating her father's words to herself—"Strength and courage. Strength and courage. Strength and courage"—Kandide kept walking, albeit still very slowly, in the direction that led away from the wolf. He seemed to be following her, but always at a distance. She began to wonder what he was doing all by himself in a place like this. *Wolves normally live in packs. Maybe there are more of them? Maybe he's waiting for his friends to show up and then he will attack me. No . . . no, he could have easily killed me back there in the cave.* She shuddered at the thought.

Except for an occasional glimpse of the wolf, Kandide could neither see nor hear another living creature. The only sound was the occasional twig cracking underfoot. Not even the wind rippled through the trees. There was only silence—deathly silence.

Maybe I should just transport out of here—to wherever I end up. But without knowing where she was, how could she even begin to set the coordinates? Transporting only worked when the Fée knew where they were starting from, as well as where they were going. She could end up anywhere or nowhere. No, she would have to find some sort of identifiable landmark first. Then she would transport. *If only I had my gaming boots,* she thought as she felt a particularly generous glob of black slimy mud ooze between her toes. *At least then I could walk faster than I'm able to with these open shoes.*

As she continued making her way through the dense forest maze, other thoughts began to consume her—thoughts of her future, the way she was treated by the Council, how much she disliked Lady Aron, how much she missed her father. *I will be healed. I will be perfect again. I will get out of here. I won't let Lady Aron win. I won't let any of them win! It is my destiny to be queen. Father said so.* Like so many vivid pictures, each image that flashed through her mind made her more and more determined to find the way out of this horrible place.

She remembered Teren talking about the Mists. "What did he say about them?" Although she knew no one would answer, it helped to hear a voice, even if it was her own. "Where are they supposed to be located? Think, Kandide, think! You're brilliant—Father has said so many times. You can figure this out. You always do."

"If only I could fly, I could see above the trees. I could find a landmark." Looking up at the tangled canopy of branches above her head, she began to chuckle at how silly she sounded. "If I could fly, I'd be gone already."

"Okay, no more *ifs*, Kandide. Father is right. *If* doesn't help solve the problem, and it certainly won't stop my wing from aching." Snapping off another branch and tossing it out of her way, Kandide flinched. The constant throbbing of her wing was bad enough, but every time she twisted a certain way, sharp pains shot up her back and into her crumpled wing. "I could certainly do without that right now." Rubbing her shoulder,

Kandide pressed on a nerve. It seemed to help lessen the pain, at least for a while.

"I could also do without this disgusting smell!" The awful stench was getting worse, and it was starting to make her feel nauseated. At least the revolting odor kept her from wanting anything to eat. "Not that there would be anything even remotely edible in these woods—except maybe me!" She shuddered at what might be out there, walking a little faster.

"Oh, yuck!" Kandide looked down just in time to stop herself from stepping in a gaseous pool of black slime. "What is that?"

Tufts of brown fur floated on the pool's oily surface. She could only imagine what lay rotting underneath. In truth, she did not want to know.

While trying to figure out the best way to go around it, she noticed what appeared to be a clearing no more than fifty meters ahead. Kandide stood there staring at it. *Could it be?*

Shafts of sunlight were illuminating some sort of an opening. Could she actually have found the edge of these dreadful woods? Her heart was racing. "I knew I could do it. I knew I could find my way! I always do!"

Careful not to fall or step into anything else that looked too slimy, Kandide made her way toward the clearing. She could hardly contain her excitement.

To her absolute amazement, she saw an immense golden gate. Its ornately patterned façade glistened in the bright sunlight. The gate was set in the middle of the highest, longest stone fence that she had ever seen. The walls appeared to stretch toward infinity in both directions. Behind them, she could just barely see the two identical towers of what looked like a magnificent castle.

"I don't know where I am," she gleefully professed, "but at least I'm somewhere!"

Curiously, as Kandide drew closer, the massive gate swung open. It was as though her arrival had been expected. *Could this be where the Banshees live?* Uncertain about entering, she briefly hesitated.

Looking back at the dark, fog-laden woods behind her, Kandide caught another glimpse of the wolf. She made her choice.

THE VEIL IN THE MISTS

"Griffins?" Kandide's eyes lit up.
As a child, she used to dream of seeing a griffin.

TWENTY-ONE

In complete contrast to where she had just been, Kandide found herself standing in an exquisitely landscaped garden. Fuchsias, hydrangeas, pansies, roses, orchids, jasmine— flowers of every kind and color filled the air with their rich fragrances. She inhaled deeply to take in their splendid aroma, hoping to clear her lungs of the stench of the Mists. Everywhere she looked, exotic botanicals formed wondrous pathways, all leading up to a magnificent golden château. Its towering spires reached upward toward the clear blue sky. Vividly colored stained glass windows sparkled in the sunlight. Even Kandide's own castle and grounds, which were truly lovely, were not so extraordinarily designed.

Kandide could only stand there, staring in wonder and awe. *What is this place? Where am I?*

The flawlessly manicured courtyard was bustling with activity. Fée from virtually every clan were busy chatting or doing chores. They were trimming shrubs, planting flowers, and going about their duties as if this were any ordinary castle. But this was no ordinary castle. It was different somehow, truly strange in its absolute perfection. Kandide could not recall ever hearing about a kingdom like this. Neither her father nor the Council had ever mentioned it.

She managed a "hello" to one young couple, who exchanged a warm greeting and then, giggling, flitted off before she could inquire as to where she was.

At least they aren't Banshees, she happily thought.

Pulling her cape tightly around her shoulders to conceal her damaged wing, Kandide started to ask another Fée where she was. He also nodded a polite greeting and then quickly flew off. Looking around, she became aware of a woman approaching. As the lady drew closer, Kandide noticed that she looked curiously familiar.

"Mother?" Kandide gasped, looking at her in disbelief.

"Kandide? Could it really be you?" the woman replied, even more astonished than Kandide.

"Yes, but—"

"I'm Selena, your mother's twin sister."

"Selena?" Kandide was stunned. "But how? I . . . I don't understand? You . . . you passed away when I was young." Bewildered, Kandide slowly looked around. Everything was so beautiful, so perfect. It all seemed real enough, but could it be that she actually hadn't survived the lightning? *Could the transport have gone wrong? Is this where Fée go when they pass on?*

Perhaps Father is here. A dozen thoughts flashed through her mind. "Then . . . does this mean that I have also passed?"

"Goodness no, child," Selena chuckled. "I assure you that you are very much alive, and so am I."

"That's a relief. I think . . ." Kandide was completely bewildered.

"My, how you've grown, and so very beautiful. How is Tiyana? How is your sister? And Teren? How is little Teren?" Selena was bubbling over with excitement and questions.

"They are all well, but—"

"And your father? How is King Toeyad? Is he well?"

"Then you haven't heard?"

"Heard? I'm afraid we don't get much news out here."

"Father has recently passed."

"Oh, Kandide, I am so very sorry. A greater leader the Fée could not have known, nor a kinder one. And now . . . why, that means you must be queen?" Selena curtsied with a deep bow. "Your Majesty!"

"Well, I . . . I'm . . ."

Kandide started to explain, but Selena continued, "Let me be the first to welcome you to the Veil of the Mists. We are so very honored. Oh dear, how rude of me. I'm just so excited to see you. Do come inside."

"Thank you. But please, Aunt Selena, call me Kandide."

"Then Kandide it is."

Kandide followed Selena through an elegant golden archway that led to the château's Great Hall. "We simply had no idea you were coming," Selena remarked most apologetically as they entered the large room, "or we would have sent a welcoming party to meet you." Looking at her torn, dirty gown and muddy shoes, she continued: "Oh dear, I do apologize. I shall have fresh clothes prepared for you immediately."

"That would be most appreciated. My trip was . . . uh . . . hastily arranged," Kandide responded, looking around at the marvelous décor.

The inside of the château was even more resplendent than its exterior. Intricately woven tapestries, majestic sculptures, and colorful paintings graced the walls. The furnishings were exquisite in every detail, masterfully carved with upholstery that was obviously the work of superior artisans. Spectacular jewels—rubies, emeralds, sapphires, and diamonds—adorned a splendidly carved marble fireplace, each catching the light with the flicker of the flames. It, too, was unlike anything she had ever seen.

"Please be seated." Selena graciously gestured toward a plush, richly embroidered chair. "I cannot believe that you are actually here in the Veil, and that you know about us. Tell me, dare I hope that the Council has amended the Articles? Can I finally visit my sister? It has been so very long. Oh dear, I am going on. With so many things I long to know, I am afraid that I am just full of questions."

"I have a few myself," Kandide responded, still gazing around the magnificently appointed hall.

"How long will you stay?" Selena was eager to know.

"My plans are, well . . . flexible," Kandide answered.

"I do hope you'll stay a while. There's so much to show you and to talk about."

"That, uh . . . is the reason I have come to visit you . . . to learn more about this place." Assuming that Selena knew nothing about her crumpled wing, Kandide decided that there was no point in telling her, at least not yet. "I'm afraid I am a bit confused, however," she continued. "I thought the Mists were only a legend—an imaginary place created to frighten young Fée into being good."

"I assure you they are quite real, and, as you undoubtedly saw outside of the Veil, quite dangerous."

"The Veil?"

"Perhaps I should start at the beginning," Selena responded, herself a little confused by Kandide's lack of knowledge about the Veil. Obviously, there was a great deal more to her niece's unexpected visit than she let on.

"Please do." Kandide tried not to seem too unaware.

"It all seems so long ago now. Your mother and I used to love to visit the meadows—"

"The meadows? Mother?" Kandide was shocked. "Mother abhors the meadows. She hasn't been there in years."

"It wasn't always so. We would often go there to gather wild berries, or to just sit under a pomegranate tree and talk—sometimes for hours. We'd then catch moonbeams to light our way home. One day, we were caught in a terrible lightning storm." Selena let her cape slide off her shoulder. "That's when my—"

Before she could finish her sentence, Kandide gasped, "Your wing, it's bent!"

"Why, yes. I thought you knew."

"You're a crumplewing? You were sent away?"

"I didn't mean to startle you. Oh dear." Selena was beside herself at the thought of upsetting her niece.

"No . . . uh . . . I'm fine. I just . . . I'm just surprised, that's all. No wonder Mother hates the meadows so," she replied, half to herself, while tying to regain her composure. "We were told you had passed—but you didn't. And now . . ." Kandide was nearly speechless by Selena's revelation. She stared at Selena's wing and simply shook her head.

"That is what your father wanted everyone to believe—that I had passed."

"But why? How? All this?" Kandide was even more perplexed.

"When the accident happened, your father could not bear to send me away. He knew that to do so would also break Tiyana's heart. Toeyad pleaded with the High Council to change the law against Imperfects. While many were willing, Lady Aron led a powerful fight to oppose it."

"Of course."

"In the end, she won by convincing enough of the Council that a vote was not even allowed. That is when your father created this sanctuary surrounded by the Mists—a secret place, where I could live in safety."

"Father created the Veil?"

"Why, yes. Although most Fée probably do not realize it, King Toeyad was quite accomplished in the wizardly arts. He didn't tell you about it?"

"Well . . . not everything," Kandide hastily replied. "He . . . his passing was rather sudden."

"I see." Realizing that there was, indeed, far more to Kandide's visit than her niece was letting on, Selena continued with a bit more explanation. "Your father created a protective

Veil around this area so that no one could transport directly in—or out, for that matter. I must say, arriving in the Mists does create quite a deterrent if you don't know where you are going."

"That it does," Kandide nodded. "So, Father built this château?"

"No. You see, at first there was just me, a small cottage, and the griffins, of course."

"Griffins?" Kandide's eyes lit up. As a child, she used to dream of seeing a griffin. Because of their proud, independent nature, her father often said that she reminded him of one. "You actually have griffins?"

"Only a few, I'm afraid," Selena replied. "Toeyad brought all that he could find here so they would be safe and we could try to restore their numbers."

"I didn't realize that there were any still alive. That is truly wonderful. I'd love to see one."

"They live up in the mountains and come down every few days for food."

"That's amazing. I hope I am still here when they do. But tell me, how . . . where did everyone else—"

"Come from? Please, have some hot tea and shortbread." As Selena was speaking, a young Fée entered with refreshments. She poured Kandide a cup of steaming hot tea. "We make it with fresh pomegranates. They are grown right here."

Almost choking at the thought of more pomegranates, Kandide managed a polite "Thank you. It sounds lovely. Do continue." Ignoring the tea, she reached for a piece of shortbread.

"I wish to know why a trumpeter of the Royal Guard was so clumsy as to step on the cape of the Crown Princess?"

TWENTY-TWO

"You asked to see me, Lady Aron?"

"Yes, do come in." She motioned for the uniformed soldier to enter the antechamber of her living quarters.

The décor in the room was a perfect reflection of Lady Aron's fiery personality; there was nothing understated in its design or color. With vivid red and orange furnishings scattered throughout, it also contained a large area rug that looked as though it was woven from actual flames.

"How may I be of service, my lady?" her visitor inquired as he stood at the edge of the carpet. He was almost afraid to step on it, lest it burn his boots.

In typical fashion, Lady Aron wasted no time getting to the point. "I wish to know why a trumpeter of the Royal Guard was so clumsy as to step on the cape of the crown princess."

"It was an unfortunate accident," the soldier responded. Slightly on the defensive, he quickly added, "I have apologized most profusely to Her Royal Highness Tiyana."

"Yes, it was an unfortunate accident, wasn't it?" She stared straight at him. "How rude of me, please be seated." Motioning toward a chair, she continued, "I just might have use for someone such as you. Tell me your name again?"

"I am called Asgart, My Lady," he answered, hesitating to sit down. He wasn't at all eager to discuss the unfortunate incident with her. "Begging your pardon, but I believe it is the same name you were given when you asked my commander about me."

"Don't be impertinent," she snapped. In spite of his boldness, Lady Aron's tone quickly softened. "Please, do be seated, Asgart. I don't bite, unless, of course, I am provoked."

"No, my lady, I mean . . . I really don't have much time." Asgart was fully aware of her bite. He had seen it from afar many times. It was not at all uncommon for her to lash out at members of her own staff for no other reason than they said "Good morning" in too cheery a tone. He quickly moved toward the door to leave, commenting, "Duty calls, you know."

"No, I don't know! I also don't know why you intentionally stepped on Kandide's cloak. And, unless you would like me to submit a report to the Council that contains . . . well, let's just say some evidence that I have recently uncovered regarding your 'malicious intent' in doing so, I suggest that you be a little more forthcoming. Now, won't you please join me in a cup of tea?" Without waiting for his answer, she poured two cups. "Sugar?"

"Just tea, thank you." Although extremely apprehensive, he sat down on the chair across from her, totally ignoring the steaming cup that she placed on the table next to him.

"So, tell me what really happened—and why."

"As I have told you, it was an accident, nothing more." Asgart was quite insistent. Lady Aron might serve on the High Council, but he was not someone to be easily intimidated, even by her. Tiyana had forgiven him, and, in his mind, that was all that mattered.

"Let me see. I know what must have happened . . ." Lady Aron tapped her left index finger on the table—a trait she often displayed when circling prey. Her large fire-agate ring flashed with color as she placed her hand on his. "You merely wanted to see if the rumors about Kandide being an Imperfect were true. Was that it, my dear?"

Quickly sliding his hand away, he was steadfast in his own defense. "I would never do anything to harm Princess Kandide!"

"Well, there certainly is no harm in wanting to know the truth about her condition, now is there? After all, you do have the right to know if your future queen is an Imperfect."

"I—"

"You don't happen to think that an Imperfect should be queen, now do you?" Lady Aron was most cajoling.

"Of course I don't, but—"

"But?"

"Please, I can say no more, my lady."

"Oh, I think you can. Tell me, are you pleased with Tara's crowning?"

"Indeed," he quickly answered with a firm nod. "She is young and inexperienced, but I have no doubt that she will be a fair and devoted leader. She is, after all, most gracious and kind."

"And Kandide is not?"

"That is not what I mean." Asgart was not at all sure how to answer such a question.

"I understand that you have had firsthand experience with Kandide's . . . shall we say, lack of graciousness."

"Respectfully, my lady, I am sure that is something you need not be concerned with. Besides, it was a very long time ago."

"My dear, dear Asgart, when it comes to you, everything is now my concern. We are going to become very good friends."

"Begging your pardon, my lady, my wife . . . uh, she will be serving dinner very soon . . . and I have yet to finish my duties. I really must be going." Asgart stood up to leave.

"Really? I'll tell you 'really'! One word from me and all of the apologies in the world will not help you. Let me hasten to say that I understand that your wife is also employed here in the castle." Lady Aron's voice suddenly shifted from intimidating to syrupy sweet. "It would be such a shame if she lost her position as well. Why, what would your two lovely children do? You wouldn't want that to happen, now, would you?"

Asgart glared at her, but before he could answer, her tone, once again, shifted, and, by the expression on her face, he knew she would not be denied. "You do understand what I'm saying, don't you, trumpeter?"

"Yes . . . yes, my lady."

"Good. Then sit!" She pointed to the chair and he grudgingly did as she requested.

"Now, tell me about what happened 'a long time ago.'" Lady Aron stared directly at him, eagerly awaiting his story.

"Well, I . . . I was a most respected guard to King Toeyad— that was until Kandide decided that I should become her aercaen partner. Even though she was young and inexperienced, she severely injured my leg in combat."

"I'm sure it was just . . . an unfortunate accident," Lady Aron chided. "Rather embarrassing, I would say."

"Well, I could have dealt with that. But to be so arrogant as to humiliate me by publicly apologizing, and then ordering her healers to fix it, right there in front of my peers, that goes beyond any sort of good gamesmanship. At least she could have let me leave the gaming field on my own accord."

Lady Aron listened with glee as he revealed what had happened.

Asgart continued: "It was Princess Kandide's first big win and she made sure everyone knew it. Then, because she felt bad about embarrassing me, she had King Toeyad make me a court trumpeter. The guys in my legion had a lot of fun with that. 'Job too tough?' they would say. 'Gone soft, have we?' I haven't been able to advance in the ranks since."

"How very unfortunate . . . for you!" Lady Aron's mind was whirling. Changing the subject, she asked, "Tell me, do you have any idea where Kandide . . . I mean Imperfects are sent? I know, in certain cases, King Toeyad seemed to have personally taken charge of that duty."

"Well, there are rumors among the guards."

"Rumors?" Lady Aron was most anxious to hear about

these rumors.

"It's probably nothing."

"I'll be the judge of that, my dear Asgart. Incidentally, now that we have become such good friends, I may be able to help get you that promotion—especially since you did act so very bravely in trying to shield Kandide from all of those pomegranates that were being hurled at her."

"I never meant for her to get hurt. I mean, I—"

"Of course you didn't." Her tone was quite patronizing. Lady Aron couldn't have been more thrilled with her latest conquest. Asgart, it seemed, was just the type of individual that she had been looking for. He was not terribly bright, but he was resolute in his feelings. And he had absolutely no loyalty to Kandide. "Please, do proceed," she prodded. "I just love rumors."

Wondering if he had already told Lady Aron too much, Asgart hesitated. "Well . . ." A promotion, however, would be more than he had dared to dream about in a very long time. *And I did stop one or two pomegranates from hitting Kandide,* he rationalized to himself. *Besides, I deserve a promotion after all I've been through.*

"Well . . .," Lady Aron urged.

"Well . . . there are rumors that King Toeyad created this secret place in an area called the Mists."

"A secret place in the Mists? So, it really does exist."

"And I just remembered something else. Your husband, Lord Aron, he may know about that place."

"Lord Aron? Why would my husband know about it?" In all her years of being married to him, she had never heard her husband mention the Mists.

"A number of years ago, I overheard King Toeyad talking with Lord Aron about a place that was safe for Imperfects to go. That's when he mentioned the Mists."

"Really? Tell me more."

"I think he said that he had created a valley . . . or did he say a veil in the Mists? I'm not sure. Anyway, I remember thinking how odd it sounded, because I always thought the Mists were just a legend. And why would Lord Aron care what happens to Imperfects?"

"Good point. Tell me, do you think you can find this secret place?"

"Uhm . . . I really wouldn't know where to look. The rumors are that the Mists cover quite a big area, and that they're a pretty dangerous place. I sure wouldn't want to go out there."

"Dangerous . . . yes, I suppose they could be dangerous. You've done well, Asgart. Tell me, what do you know about garglans?"

Looking from Jake to her niece,
Selena could not help but notice the instant
attraction they had for each other.

TWENTY-THREE

"**P**lease have some more shortbread." Selena offered her niece another of the freshly baked biscuits.

Kandide eagerly accepted it, eating one, then another, and another, until she had almost finished the entire plate. Never could she remember anything tasting so good. Her energy was even beginning to return.

"They are quite delicious," Kandide replied, half apologizing as she eyed the last remaining piece. "I must get the recipe for our pastry chef."

"I'm glad you like them. Margay will be thrilled."

"Margay?"

"She oversees the kitchen. Her biscuits and pastries are truly incredible. Now, let's see, where was I in my story? Oh, yes. Shortly after arriving here, I was searching in the woods for wild mushrooms when I met Jake."

"Did I hear my name?" A tall, extremely handsome Fée bounded into the room. With tousled black hair and vibrant green eyes that seemed to sparkle even brighter when he spotted Kandide, Jake had a boyish smile that she instantly found irresistible. He acknowledged her with a highly flirtatious "Hello." Kandide could have sworn that he actually winked at her.

"Jake," Selena motioned for him to join them, "I would like you to meet my niece, Her Majesty Queen Kandide. Kandide, this is Jake."

"Uh . . . Oh . . . Qu . . . Queen Kandide?" Jake's jaw dropped almost as low as his very formal bow. He managed to stammer out an embarrassed, but certainly more appropriate, greeting. "Your Majesty, begging your pardon. I . . . I . . . I didn't realize . . ."

"No apology necessary," a smiling Kandide replied in her most regal tone. Offering him her hand, she added with a smile, "It is my pleasure, I'm sure." She continued by extending him an invitation that sounded more like a command. "Do join us."

As though he had been hit by a block of cement, Jake dropped into the nearest chair. *She's so beautiful,* he thought, his eyes barely leaving Kandide's.

Looking from Jake to her niece, Selena could not help but notice the instant attraction they felt for each other. "Well, now that we have the formalities out of the way, may I continue with my story?"

"Please do," Kandide responded. She was also having trouble looking away from Jake. Never had she seen such

JAKE

beautiful eyes—*except my own, of course,* she thought. Jake was the most mesmerizing Fée she had ever met. He had an almost impish charm juxtaposed with a spirited sense of complete inner confidence. And that incredible smile—it made her feel as though he could ease the entire world of all its ills.

"As I was saying," Selena continued, "I was walking in the woods one afternoon when this . . . this Jake fellow came bounding out."

"He seems to do a lot of that," Kandide interjected with a slight chuckle.

Blushing, Jake only slightly protested, "I . . . uh . . ."

"Yes, it does seem to be a trait of his." Selena looked over at him and smiled. "Jake also had to leave his clan."

"Why? You're so . . . so perfect." Realizing what she had just said, Kandide began to blush as well. "I mean . . ."

An approving smile crossed Jake's face as he leaned back in his chair. "Not really," he modestly replied.

"Jake was a victim of the after-wars that happened following the unification of the clans," Selena explained.

"But I thought . . . I'm confused." Kandide's focus slowly shifted away from Jake to Selena, who continued to speak.

"We were quick to brag about how few Fée were killed during the clan unification battles, but many hundreds of others were badly injured—both during and after the war. Continual outbreaks of fighting went on for years. Jake was attempting to stop a rumble that had turned particularly violent, when a burning log fell on his legs."

"See!" Jake suddenly flew straight up. His boots, however, remained on the floor.

Kandide could only stare at him in stunned disbelief. "I . . . what . . .?"

"I lost my feet. I'm special, too! Bet you wouldn't have known it, though. It took years to develop feet that work like real ones. Now we've figured out how to do arms, and legs, and—"

"Can you do wings?" Kandide asked, almost too eagerly.

"Not perfectly yet, but we do have a prototype," Jake answered with a great deal of pride. "Want to see it? I can show it to you."

Abruptly, the realization of Jake's lack of feet struck Kandide. As he continued to flutter above her head, it took all of her composure not to appear repulsed. Nevertheless, she managed a polite reply. "If I'm still here. I do have a kingdom to run, you know." She then hastened to ask Selena, in almost a whisper, "Father sent the rest here as well?"

"No, not in the beginning. Jake told me that there were others who were also injured and living in the Mists. And while they should have been able to return from the fighting with honor and glory, they were instead 'discreetly' sent away. Many of them did eventually join us. Unfortunately, many others were never found. Still more were too far gone for anyone to help, and simply would not leave the woods. We don't know what happened to them, but we fear the worst."

"But . . ." Kandide was not sure how she felt about what she was hearing. "They were Imperfects, and yet they were injured because they joined with Father to help unite the clans and end the fighting. In a way, I suppose they are heroes, and yet . . ."

"In a way? You suppose? You bet they are heroes," Jake insisted, rather astonished at how she could even question the fact.

"Well, I'm not sure that sending them away was the right thing to do, Jake," Kandide added with a slightly defensive undertone, "but what else could be done with them? I mean . . . they could hardly live among the rest of us. It just wouldn't be right."

"No, I suppose 'it just wouldn't be right,' Your Majesty!" he retorted, mimicking her words. *You may be Calabiyau's queen,* he thought as he stared at her from his chair, *but it's a good thing your rule doesn't extend to the Veil.*

Breaking what seemed like an interminable silence, Kandide, rather matter-of-factly, attempted to justify her remarks. "I mean, it's in our Articles, Jake. Even Father wasn't able to get the High Council to change that."

"And that is exactly why King Toeyad granted the Veil its independence—so that we govern ourselves and aren't subject to the Articles of Calabiyau or its rulers!" There was a great deal of innuendo in Jake's voice.

"Yes, and that was very wise of Father—to create a safe place for Imperfects to live." Becoming bored with his insinuations, Kandide instantly turned her attention back to her aunt. "So, then what happened, Selena?"

"We began building this château and the surrounding village," she replied.

"Imperfects built this?" Kandide blurted out, amazed at how they could have possibly built something so beautiful.

Her astonishment, combined with her callous, arrogant attitude, offended Jake even more. "And why not?" His tone was highly perturbed, and then, as though remembering Kandide's stature, he emphatically added, "Your Majesty! We may be missing feet, or have crumpled wings—some of us have even lost a leg or an arm—all so that you and your kind can live in a land that is safe. But we certainly aren't helpless—or useless!" With a hurried, albeit grudgingly respectful bow, Jake started to leave, turning back only to add, "By your leave, Your Majesty, my duties require me elsewhere."

Kandide was not sure if it was Jake's audacity or what he was saying that disturbed her more. As her eyes followed him out of the room, her face surely revealed the conflict.

"He isn't perfect, but then is anybody?"

TWENTY-FOUR

"Jake is very proud of all we have accomplished, and with good reason," Selena interjected in an attempt to soften his behavior. "It was he who persuaded most of the Fée who were living in the Mists to come here. He convinced them that they are worthwhile and could live normal and productive lives, full of love and joy."

"But how can he be so happy? I mean . . . he . . . he doesn't have any . . . well, you know, feet!"

"He isn't perfect, but then is anybody?"

Kandide started to answer, "I cer—" Thinking better of it, she sank back down into her chair. "It's all so confusing, so very confusing."

"To one clan, perfection is being tall, to another it is being short, and to yet another it is being fair or dark. Some are smarter than others, some are more clever or creative. Your mother and I are green, while you are pale like your father. We are all different. But all Fée, whether they are born with challenges or become permanently injured, have something to offer, Kandide, if only they are given a chance to develop and utilize their individual talent and skill."

"Are you saying that every Fée living here is . . . is . . . an Imperfect?"

"Well, we don't use that term, but yes, I guess we are."

"What are they . . . uh . . . called?"

"Oh, let's see, that's Salara over there with Ilene and Robbi. And there's Jessita and Margrite. We all have names. Granted, each of us has different ways in which we are able to excel, but we all work and contribute as we can."

Pulling her cloak tightly around her shoulders, Kandide, in her most congenial way, responded, "I see. So, how do you live? Where do you get food?"

"We grow all of our food, and only eat food that is grown. We respect all life."

"It's most amazing. I mean, truly wonderful."

"I was hoping that you had come to learn about us, and to help convince the Council that we are all valuable. But I am sensing that is not the case."

"Uh . . . yes. Of course that is why I am here." Kandide's uneasiness was fully apparent to Selena.

Selena observed her niece for a few moments, and then, placing her hands on the tabletop, stood up, commenting, "Good, then let me take you on a tour while there is still daylight."

"That would be lovely."

TWENTY-FIVE

The entire High Council was in an uproar. Lady Aron was, as usual, the most vocal. "You simply must tell us where Kandide is, Tiyana. The seasons must change or all life will be in peril."

"I have told you, I sent her away." Tiyana was adamant in her response. "There is nothing that can be done right now."

"There is always something that can be done," the fiery Council member retorted, almost too calmly. Her golden eyes seemed to hold some hidden secret. "Toeyad gave you his last kiss and, with it, at least some of the Gift. If you cannot find Kandide, then the solution is simple: You must use what you have been given to trigger the Frost." Her tone, as usual, was entirely matter-of-fact.

"While I hate to agree with Lady Aron," Lady Batony interjected with a sigh of resignation, "I am afraid, Tiyana, that you may be our only hope."

All were surprised with Lady Batony's concurrence with Lady Aron in this matter, especially since the consequences of deploying the Gift could be fatal to Tiyana. The feuding between these two Council members was legendary. At times, it had been so obnoxious that it seemed as though they actually sought out reasons to disagree.

Tara looked angrily from Council member to Council member. "You are supposed to be my mother's friends—all of you! How can any of you even suggest such a thing, especially you, Lady Batony?"

Although she did not want to be queen, and was extremely uncomfortable in her new role, Tara was, nevertheless, crowned. Not only was she untrained for the position, but also, her free spirit and gentle ways simply could not command the type of respect that her title demanded. Not until now, that is.

Looking rather sheepish, Lady Batony stammered, "Well, I . . . I mean . . . it might be our only hope. Oh, dear, if only Kandide had not gone to the meadows. I remember when I was a little girl—"

"But you are not a little girl," Tara cut her off, "and Kandide did go to the meadows. As Father would say, 'It is today that we must deal with, nothing else.'"

Proud of her daughter, Tiyana placed her hand on Tara's shoulder. "And how we deal with the consequences is what will determine our destiny."

"That is quite true, Tiyana," Lady Aron abruptly interjected. "And as you well know, the consequences of not triggering the Frost will most assuredly be fatal."

"So could Mother's attempt to deploy it!" Tara's vehemence was both a surprise and a welcome show of strength from the young queen.

Standing, Lady Aron continued speaking in her normal icy tone: "We all realize the price Tiyana might pay, but each of us must pass at one time or another. And since it appears that we won't be seeing Kandide again, it is the greater good that we must all think of now."

"Well, I've had just about enough of your greater good, Lady Aron." Tara slammed her hand down on the broad arm of her crystal throne chair. "You may be of the Fire clan, but it is ice that is in your heart. The High Council is dismissed—until I call you back!"

"How dare you!" a startled and very indignant Lady Aron fired back.

"How dare I? Well, as your queen, I . . . I . . . I command it!" For the first time since her crowning, Tara was assuming at least some semblance of authority. She glared at each of the Council members. "I said you are dismissed! All of you!"

"Bravo, Tara!" All eyes instantly shifted to Teren, who had just entered the chamber. Realizing his brazenness, the young prince quickly melted back into the corner of the room. "I mean, Your Majesty."

"Why, thank you, Teren." She smiled at him, and then turned her attention back to the Council members. "Well?"

Grumbling, they filed out of the chamber. Only Tara, Teren, and their mother remained.

"After what you just told us, I'm even more concerned about Lady Aron's comment that we won't be seeing Kandi again. You don't think . . . ?"

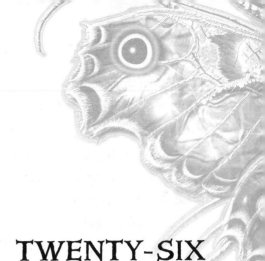

TWENTY-SIX

"**P**erhaps the others are right, Tara. I have lived a good life, and the seasons must change. I am sure that I have enough of your father's essence to trigger the Frost. It just may have to do."

"I won't let you, Mother!" Teren jumped up, his hands squarely on his hips.

"We won't let you, Mother." Tara was equally insistent. "You may be able to change the seasons this year, but if you pass, what happens after that? Please, tell us about Kandide. Where did you send her? We must be able to find her."

"She has to be somewhere!" Teren persisted.

"I cannot let you go in search of her—either of you. Tara, you are queen, and the Council needs your wisdom and caring more than ever right now."

"Then I'll go alone," Teren insisted.

"May the earthly spirits help us if something should happen to you, Teren. Lady Aron would be next in line for the throne."

"What?" They both answered, astounded by her words.

"Why?" The look on Teren's face was more than just surprise. He was completely taken aback by his mother's words. "I don't understand."

"It was a long time ago," Tiyana began explaining. "Part of the preliminary treaty negotiations with the clans included Lady Aron marrying your father. The leaders felt that if the Fire and Water clans were united, the other clans would join rank. Everyone knew that there would never be any sort of peace until those two clans stopped their fighting. There was just one problem: Toeyad would not agree to marry her. As king, he had that authority. Your father and I met not long after his refusal, so, of course, it then became all my fault."

"No wonder she's so nasty to you, Mother," Tara remarked.

"According to your father, she has always been extremely malevolent—even as a child—and has never changed."

"Father knew her as a young girl?" Teren quizzed.

"Yes. Firenza—Lady Aron—used to come with her parents to the clan conclaves that were held here in the castle. In spite of the fighting, the meetings went on for decades before the treaty negotiations started and the High Council was formed. Evidently, she was quite the bully, even back then, always picking on the other children and causing them to get in trouble. Of course, if she got caught, Toeyad said she would lie and place the blame on one of her playmates."

"Of course," Tara nodded. "It's no different today."

"No, not really," Tiyana replied. "It was even rumored that Firenza betrayed her own brother to a Banshee raiding party, simply because she felt that their father paid too much attention to him."

"I didn't know she even had a brother," Teren frowned. "That's horrible. What happened to him?"

"No one knows."

"Didn't anyone suspect her of being involved?" Tara knew Lady Aron could be nasty, but betraying her own brother to the Banshees? That she couldn't even begin to comprehend.

"Some did suspect, but, naturally, Lady Aron denied having anything to do with it. Your father, however, overheard her talking about it to one of her friends—who, coincidentally, mysteriously disappeared a few weeks later, near that same area."

"How come Father didn't say anything?" Teren questioned.

"He did, but Firenza's parents were extremely protective of their 'little girl,' and things were in such turmoil back then, with the clan wars, that nothing ever came of it."

"Yeah, and she's still getting away with murder—so to speak," Tara sighed.

"Yeah, well, I still don't understand." Teren looked quizzically at his mother. "How come she's next in line for the throne?"

"Over the years, Lady Aron grew more and more powerful in her own clan. I'm sure it was because most of the clan leaders were afraid of her."

"Like now." It was clear that Tara was referring to several of their own Council members.

"But I still don't see—" Teren pressed.

"In order to create some semblance of harmony—and to

get the Fire clan to sign the treaty—Toeyad compromised by agreeing that if he died without any heirs, she would inherit the Gift and become the ruling queen."

"That's a scary thought!"

"And I'm sure, Teren, many felt the same way, even back then. But faced with more clan fighting, it probably seemed like the lesser of two evils. You must remember, Lady Aron has always commanded a certain following."

Teren shook his head. "Well, certain following or not, no way will I ever let her become queen!"

"And after what you just told us," Tara interjected, "I'm even more concerned about Lady Aron's comment that we won't be seeing Kandi again. You don't think . . . ?"

"Her comment was a bit odd," Tiyana agreed. "However, I cannot possibly see how she can know about the . . ."

"Know about what, Mother? Please, you must tell us," Tara pleaded. "If Lady Aron is up to something, and she finds Kandi first, who knows what she'll do?"

"Lady Aron may be abrasive, but even she knows that the Gift must be deployed by Kandide, and that if it were to be transferred to someone else, your sister must give it willingly. For that reason alone, I cannot believe that she will do anything to harm her."

"You don't know that, Mother. We need to find Kandi—and soon," Tara insisted. "Who knows what Lady Aron would do to convince her to 'willingly' transfer the Gift?"

"I suppose you are right, at least about finding Kandide. Please be seated, my children, I have a story to tell you. It happened when you were both quite small . . ." Reluctantly, Tiyana revealed the story of Selena and the secret of the Mists.

Tara and Teren listened intently to their mother's words, asking question after question.

"And you haven't seen Aunt Selena or been to the Veil since?" Tara queried.

"No, Tara. And no one must ever learn of this place," Tiyana warned. "Knowledge of it could destroy everything your father and I worked so very hard to achieve. There are already too many rumors circulating about the Mists."

"We understand, Mother," Tara nodded.

"Well, I'm going there to find her."

"Teren . . ."

"I'll be okay, Mother. I am a magi, you know."

Tara was equally insistent. "It's the only way, Mother."

"And the sooner I get started, the better!" Teren sounded more grown-up than ever. "Tara, you'd better call the High Council back so you can tell them that you've decided to send me to go look for Kandide."

"Will do, little brother!"

"But, Teren, I'm still . . ."

"Like Tara said, it's the only way, Mother. You have to send me there."

"Blind? She's blind?"
Kandide was stunned. She had never met
anyone who was blind.

TWENTY-SEVEN

"It's all so very hard to imagine," Kandide exclaimed as she and Selena began their tour. There was a note of amazement in her voice. They walked through an elaborately carved doorway that led to the château's long gathering hall. It was full of Fée from many different clans. All were engaged in various types of activities. Some were weaving, some were sewing, and still others carved, painted, or sculpted.

The more Kandide saw, the more remarkable it seemed that Imperfects—the Fée who had always repulsed her—could create such an extraordinary place. "So what you are telling me, Selena, is that all of this, everything, was created by Imper—um . . . I mean, the Fée who live here?"

"Yes, my child, everything. Not only do we grow our own food, we quarried and carved all of the stone that built this château. We are completely self-sustaining. We make all of our own pottery and furniture, and we weave and dye our own cloth."

"That is amazing, truly amazing." Looking around, Kandide noticed a very attractive young Fée with long dark-brown braids that fell past her waist. Her skin was the color of milk chocolate, and she was dressed in delicate shades of blue, teal, and pink, with elegant bejeweled silver spirals in her hair. Her wings were large and flowing, and shimmered in the perfect reflection of the colors in her dress.

At first glance, she, at least, appeared to be quite normal. "What's wrong with her? Uh . . . I mean, she seems to be perf— I mean . . . What is her name?" Kandide stammered.

"She is called Leanne. Come. Let me introduce you to her." Kandide followed her aunt over to the young, pretty Fée. "Leanne, I would like you to meet my niece, Her Majesty Queen Kandide."

"Your Majesty?" Leanne curtsied. "I . . . I . . . didn't realize you—"

"It's all right, Leanne. There is no reason why you should have. Her visit was totally unexpected." Turning to Kandide, Selena continued, "Leanne is a healer. Her Talents are some of the most remarkable I have ever seen. Given time, she has been able to help—if not completely heal—almost every type of ailment. She has even worked wonders with certain types of extremely severe injuries."

"Really? I mean . . . that is wonderful, Leanne. It is my pleasure to meet someone with so much of the Talent." Kandide extended her hand.

LEANNE

Leanne, however, did not reach out to take it, instead replying, "Thank you, Your Majesty. I shall know your voice now."

"And we shall see you tonight at dinner, Leanne," Selena interjected. "I want to finish Kandide's tour before it gets too much later. I am sure she would like to rest and freshen up before dinner."

"Of course." Leanne graciously bowed to Kandide, adding, "I look forward to it, Your Majesty."

"As do I." Kandide nodded.

"Then shall we continue, Kandide?" Selena turned to depart.

Hurrying after her, Kandide whispered, "What did Leanne mean, she'll know my voice?"

"Leanne is without sight. Although some say she sees far better than anyone here."

"Blind? She's blind?" Kandide was stunned. She had never met anyone who was blind. "Then how can she heal?"

"Goodness, child, it is her gift, that's how. Her talent is truly amazing. I would have never thought it possible, but she has actually been able to help heal my wings. They were far worse."

"Really?" Kandide was extremely eager to hear more.

"Yes. Although I am not convinced, Leanne thinks that one day she might be able to make them completely straight. I can actually fly short distances now. I won't let her work on me as often as she'd like, though."

"Why not? I mean, if she can make you perfect again, Aunt Selena?"

"Perfection takes many forms, my child. Not all of them are

in the shape of a wing, or an arm, or a foot. Besides, healing an old injury takes far too much of her strength. There are so many others here who truly need her help. She has, however, had excellent results with wings that are only recently damaged."

"How recently?" Kandide tried not to sound overly curious.

"Well, naturally, the sooner the better. Even after a few days, she can sometimes make a huge difference. Of course, it depends upon the severity of the injury."

Seeing Jake, Selena called to him, "Jake. Jake, why don't you show Kandide what you have been doing with your prototype wings?"

With a slight bow and a bit of an ungracious undertone, he replied, "I'm sure Her Majesty is far too busy to worry about things like artificial wings."

"Oh, but I'm not . . . too busy, that is." Then, to arrest his sarcasm even further, she added, "I am very interested in what everyone here is doing."

"How . . . how very amiable of you, Your Majesty." Still annoyed at Kandide's earlier comments, Jake half-heartedly bowed again. "Then it would be my pleasure to show you our inventions."

"Please, call me Kandide." She returned his bow by nodding her head ever so slightly.

"As you wish . . . Kandide." His words still carried a tinge of mockery.

"Oh dear," Selena interrupted, more to defuse the brash undertones of Jake's behavior than because of the time, "it is getting late and there is so much more to see. Perhaps the rest of the tour should happen tomorrow. Kandide, you must be very tired. May I show you to your room? I'm sure you will want to relax a bit before supper. Tomorrow we shall have a gala feast in your honor."

"That sounds lovely." Kandide was still looking at Jake. "And I certainly would like to freshen up."

"I shall have a hot bath drawn for you, immediately. I am afraid that your room is not quite what you are used to, but it is well appointed and warm." Selena could not help but notice that Kandide and Jake were staring at each other again. "Shall we?"

"Oh . . . yes." She turned her attention back to her aunt. "And I'm sure that my room will do quite nicely." Looking back at Jake, she asked, "You will be joining us for dinner, won't you, Jake?"

"I have to eat . . ." With a shrug and another mockingly deep bow that included an elaborate flourish, he added, "Kandide."

Not to be outdone, she gestured for him to rise. "Then, please, stand up before you injure your back." Abruptly turning to Selena, Kandide added, "Shall we go? I really am feeling a bit tired just now, and that hot bath sounds wonderful." A self-satisfied grin crossed Kandide's face as she walked away from Jake. He is so very handsome, she thought to herself. Pity about his feet.

Walking toward the château, Selena offhandedly commented, "It would appear that Jake is quite enamored with you."

Kandide stood up, nervously straightening her dress. "You won't tell anyone, will you? Please? Don't tell Jake!"

TWENTY-EIGHT

"Me? Jake? Enamored with me?" To Kandide, the thought was unbelievable. "Why, he doesn't have any fee—uh . . . feelings for me. That is well apparent!"

"Feet he may not have, but feelings, I would not be so sure," Selena persisted as they entered Kandide's sleeping chamber.

Her aunt was right about the room. Although bright and cheery, it was not at all what Kandide was accustomed to. *It doesn't even have an antechamber,* she thought, as if to minimize her astonishment at all that they had achieved in this amazing land. *But then, it was designed by Imperfects.*

The chamber's neatly appointed furnishings were upholstered in delicate pinks and soft mint greens. Sunlight streamed through an arched window that overlooked the gardens, and there was a large vase of freshly cut pink and green ginger blossoms sitting on the dressing table. Their spicy exotic fragrance filled the air.

At least the bed looks comfortable, Kandide thought as she glanced around the room. With big fluffy pillows and perfectly turned-down satin sheets, the bed was, indeed, an inviting sight. Only that morning, she hadn't been sure she would ever enjoy a hot bath and a good night's sleep again. Suddenly feeling extremely tired, Kandide yawned. "Oh dear, please excuse me, Aunt Selena, it's been a long day."

"Not at all, my dear. You must be exhausted. May I hang up your cloak?" Selena reached for the garment. "I am afraid we have no ladies-in-waiting here."

"No, thank you, I . . ." But Kandide spoke too late; Selena had already removed the cape from her shoulders. Kandide's crumpled wing was exposed.

"I see," Selena gently responded, not at all surprised by the revelation. She knew something was not right, almost from the moment Kandide had arrived. "So this is why you are here, my child."

"That's not true! I'm . . . I'm . . . I'm not an Imperfect! I . . . I . . . am queen!" Kandide grabbed the cape from her aunt. "You don't understand. I'm . . . I'm not like them, Selena. I'm not! I'm just not!"

But even Kandide could not deny the reflection of her twisted, crumpled wing in the mirror that hung above the dressing table. With the reality of the situation staring her in the face, every ounce of adrenaline that she had mustered to appear stately and normal instantly drained away. It was as though all of the things that had happened over the past few days hit her at once. The accident, the shame, the exhaustion, her own mother sending her away—everything collided at that very moment.

Her purple-blue eyes filled with tears. "They called me a crumplewing, Selena—Kandi Crumplewing! Can you imagine? I am their queen!" Kandide collapsed into a nearby chair. "Oh, Selena, what am I going to do?" Pain shot through her back and shoulder, and her wing was throbbing worse than ever. "What am I going to do?"

Putting her arms around her niece, Selena tried to comfort her. "Hush now, it's all right. Everything is going to be all right, Kandide. Of course you are queen, and a very beautiful one."

Pulling away from her aunt, Kandide abruptly sat up. "No. No, Selena, it's not all right. It was Mother who sent me away! She's ashamed of me now. It's not enough that I'm so beautiful. Perfection is what really matters. You know that. My own subjects laughed at me when they saw my wing. They almost killed me. Everyone abhors me now—especially Mother!" Kandide began sobbing. "Mother is ashamed of me—she hates me!"

"Tiyana doesn't hate you, Kandide. And no one here cares whether your wing is perfect or not. Outside, the world can be very cruel. Here, in the Veil, it is what's inside that matters. Come now, dry those beautiful eyes." Selena handed her niece a handkerchief from the dresser. "You'll stay here with us."

Suddenly struck by that idea, Kandide looked up. "With Imperfe—I mean, I can't! I . . . I couldn't stand . . . No . . . No, I must go away. Right now!" Kandide stood up, nervously straightening her dress. "You won't tell anyone, will you? Please? Don't tell Jake!" She clutched Selena's hands, half pleading, half commanding her not to reveal her secret. "Please don't tell Jake, Selena. I'll . . . I'll be gone as soon as I can fix my face. Just . . . just say I had to return home."

"As you wish, my child," Selena took her hand. "But only if you promise me that you will not leave until tomorrow."

"I . . . I can't go down to dinner. Not now!"

"I'll make your excuses and have your dinner sent up. Perhaps you will consider letting Leanne take a look at your wi—"

"No!" Kandide was emphatic. "No one else must know."

"Leanne is very discreet. She will not reveal your secret. We can merely say that you are tired and have come down with a headache from all of your travels."

"You completely trust her? Do you think she might heal me? I . . . I . . . just don't know."

"It's worth a try. Shall I ask her to come up?"

"You won't say why?" Realizing that her plea sounded more like an order than a request, Kandide quickly caught herself and softened her tone. "I mean, you will command her to secrecy?"

"I will inform her of your wishes. Now rest a bit. I'll be back in a few minutes."

Having regained her composure, Kandide was adamant. "I'm leaving tomorrow, no matter what."

"As you wish," Selena shrugged. With a knowing sigh, she left to find Leanne.

TWENTY-NINE

Alone in her room, Kandide tried to straighten her wing, but it was simply too badly damaged and the pain was unbearable each time she tried. As she stood there staring at herself in the mirror, more of her father's words came back to her: "It is your destiny to be a great queen, Kandide."

Sitting back down in the neatly upholstered chair, she began remembering the times when she was a young girl and her father taught her lessons in self-reliance. He would take her to various places in the forest around their castle and insist that she find the way home. *Of course, I always did,* she thought. *Just like I found my way here.* A faint smile crossed her lips as she remembered how proud King Toeyad had always been when she would finally spot the castle's main tower above the trees.

Then there was the time when he first challenged her to partake in the battle games with the Royal Guard. Even though she returned covered with bumps and bruises, she did it. She learned to fight—and *very* well!

Kandide's spirits picked up a bit as she reminisced about that day. It seemed so very long ago when King Toeyad sat her upon his knee, and, with a big hug and a smile, remarked, "You are learning well, my daughter. You have shown the strength and the courage that you will need to realize your destiny. My sympathies to your opponent, when next you compete."

Despite her bruises, Kandide's response was as proud as if she had just defeated his entire army. "You should see him now, Father!"

"That's it!" Jumping up, Kandide was almost ecstatic for the first time since the accident. "Father's words ... Leanne will heal my wing and I will fulfill my destiny. Father has said so!"

Again she glanced in the mirror at her wing. This time her reaction was very different. "I will be perfect again. I will! Then I will show them ... I'll show them all. Even Mother will be proud of me."

THIRTY

"So, she isn't coming to dinner?" Jake responded after having been told of Kandide's headache. He was standing in the hall just outside the large main dining room. "I'll just bet she has a headache. Too good for us, she is. Well, it's her loss. I can't stand her kind, anyway."

"Now, Jake," Selena urged, "remember, we don't judge here, even if the handicap is ignorance or prejudice."

"Or both! Besides, she's the one who judges—just because she's so perfect. She's not all that great looking anyway."

"You could be a little forgiving as well, Jake. Kandide was raised to be queen, you know."

"Yeah, and it's a good thing she's not our queen!"

"In any case, have you seen Leanne? I thought she might be able to help with Kandide's headache."

"Maybe she can help with her attitude!" Jake turned to go into the dining hall.

Shaking her head, Selena softly replied, "Maybe . . ."

THIRTY-ONE

Within a few minutes, Kandide heard a knock at her door. Holding her cape tightly around her shoulders, she cautiously opened it. Selena and Leanne entered.

"Your Majesty," Leanne curtsied. "Selena tells me you require my assistance."

"Yes. I command you . . . I mean . . . I understand that you may be able to help me." Defensive, yet regal, Kandide tried to hide her anguish.

"I have had some luck with wings, and, although I cannot promise, I am honored to try."

"You've already told her?" Kandide exclaimed.

"Give her a chance," Selena responded with a reassuring tone.

"How many others know? I . . . I must leave."

"If that is what you truly wish, but I do think you should let her try."

"Please let me try, Your Majesty," Leanne implored.

"But you are blind. I mean . . ."

"I understand how you feel. It's okay. I heal with my hands, not my eyes."

"What if it doesn't work?" Kandide was still extremely defensive.

"What if it does?" Selena was starting to become impatient with Kandide's attitude. "Let her try, child." Her insistence gave Kandide the sense of security she needed to temper her desperation.

Becoming excited again, Kandide's attitude instantly changed. "Do you really think it might work?"

"We won't know until we try." Leanne placed both hands on Kandide's wing and instantly felt the pain and torment that she had suffered. She became intimately aware of the horrible disfigurement that occurred when the lightning struck. Kandide felt Leanne's immense power starting to flow through her body. Slightly painful, it seemed to pulse and tingle at the same time. To her amazement, within seconds, Kandide's wing became straight and beautiful.

"You've done it, Leanne. I'm perfect again!" Looking in the mirror, Kandide was elated. "I'm perf—"

Shortly after Leanne stopped channeling, however, Kandide's wing began to crumple again.

"Do it again!" Kandide ordered, still excited about the success of the first attempt.

Again, her wing straightened, and then deformed a few seconds after Leanne took her hands away. Growing paler and paler, Leanne kept trying, but each time her channeling stopped, Kandide's wing returned to its crumpled state. Exhausted and weak, she started to try once more.

"That is enough for now, Leanne." Selena stopped her from attempting it again.

"Why are you stopping her?" Kandide insisted with a strong sense of indignation.

Looking at her niece, Selena firmly responded, "Kandide, Leanne is exhausted. She can try again later, when her strength returns."

"She must do it now! I want her to heal me now!"

"Kandide, please, it may take several treatments." Selena was not at all happy with her niece's ungrateful insistence.

Kandide's disappointment turned into near rage. "I knew it wouldn't work! How dare you come in here with your promises! How dare you get my hopes up!"

"Begging your pardon, Your Majesty, I am very sorry," Leanne apologized. "You were so badly injured that it may well take more strength than I have at one time. We can, however, continue treatments a little each day. I am positive that I will eventually be able to heal your wing."

"Go away! Go away! You're . . . you're nothing but an . . . an Imperfect! And now, so am I!" Kandide fell onto the bed sobbing. All of the pain and humiliation that she had kept pent up inside simply poured out all at once. "There is no hope. You lied to me. Father lied to me. I have no destiny. Leave me!" She was all but screaming. "Both of you, leave me!"

"Your Majesty—" Leanne tried to calm her.

Kandide sat up and glared straight at Leanne, shouting, "Go! I command it. I want to be alone!"

"As you wish, Kandide." Selena was quickly losing patience with her niece's reprehensible behavior. She took Leanne's arm and they left the room. A sad frown crossed Selena's face as she paused for a moment before slowly closing the bedroom door and leaving Kandide, as she had requested, alone.

"I'm so sorry to have failed her, Selena," Leanne sighed, shaking her head.

"Right now, the only failure is deep within Kandide. Her pride, along with her anger, has consumed her reason. With time, I am sure she will see things in their proper perspective."

"I know how difficult it is for her. I remember when I first lost my sight. I, too, was angry."

"Yes, but then you, Leanne, have always had an extraordinary spirit. I fear Kandide is not so blessed."

"I only wish that I—"

"There will be other days."

"I'm sure I can eventually help her, Selena."

"I'm not so sure. Kandide's wing is not her most serious problem."

The two of them walked down the stairs to the dining room with Leanne still insisting that she could ultimately heal Kandide. "Perhaps we can find others to channel even more power. I almost had enough; I could feel it."

"You've done all you can for her right now. Let's have dinner. I'll have a meal sent up to Kandide a little later."

"So, her headache isn't cured?" Jake chided, seeing Leanne

and Selena without Kandide. "Our queen won't be gracing us for dinner after all? She just can't stand being around us, can she? Well, too bad!"

"Jake, please," Selena urged. "You don't understand."

"No, Selena, you don't understand. We live in our world; she is one of them."

"Perhaps," Selena quietly responded. "Perhaps."

"As glad as I am that Kandide is gone, I am very concerned about the Frost."

THIRTY-TWO

"You seem unusually chipper, my dear." Lord Aron was standing with his wife on the balcony outside their suite of rooms in the castle. It was a warm, beautiful December evening. The sun was just beginning to set over the lake near the edge of the courtyard grounds.

"The red and amber reflections in the water truly complement you," he continued, looking out across the horizon and then back to her. "Even the jewels in your gown seem to capture the fiery tones in this evening's sky."

"That they do," Lady Aron answered with an overly endearing manner, "and you have always loved these colors on me."

"I don't believe I have ever seen you in anything else," he teased, taking her hand and softly kissing it. Lord Aron had fallen in love with his wife the instant he saw her.

"Well, lavender is hardly my color," she responded with an overly flirtatious grin. Throughout their marriage, she could be warm and loving one minute, and as cold as ice the next.

"What is making you so very happy tonight?"

"Why wouldn't I be, my darling? We no longer have to put up with that wretched creature."

"Am I to assume that you are referring to Kandide?" He put his arms around her waist. A gentle breeze fanned the air, and, from the courtyard below, the lilting strains of a harpist could be heard.

She responded by laying her head against his shoulder. "And who else could I possibly be referring to?"

"That is very unkind, even for you, my dear."

"Is it?" Lady Aron looked up at him, her amber eyes slowly turning away to face the sunset. "Even you must admit that Kandide's behavior was arrogant and self-centered beyond all reason."

Turning his wife's face back, he looked directly at her and winked. "She has her rivals."

"She may have, but I certainly do not." Lady Aron winked back. "My concern right now, however, is for the Gift. As glad as I am that Kandide is gone, I am very concerned about the Frost."

"As we all are, my dear. I don't think Tiyana thought about the Gift when she sent Kandide away. I'm quite sure she was more interested in merely trying to save her daughter's life."

"You bring up a very good point. Fool that Tiyana is, it just doesn't make sense that she . . ."

"That she what?"

"That she would just blindly send her daughter away like that."

"You're getting at something, Firenza."

Putting her arms around her husband's neck, Lady Aron's smile was almost genuine. "You know me so well, my darling. But time is truly running out. I don't even want to think of the consequences if the Gift is not deployed—and soon. We must do something to find Kandide. She must be convinced to transfer the Gift."

"Kandide will never transfer the Gift."

"Perhaps she will have no choice."

"What do you mean?"

"There are ways of persuading her." A chilling glee crept into Lady Aron's voice.

"Persuade how?" Lord Aron removed her arms from around his neck. He had always known that his wife was in love with King Toeyad, and that she married him out of spite when Kandide was born. It was a fact that had contributed greatly to her immense dislike of the crown princess. Lord Aron had hoped that with the birth of their son, things would be different, and for a time they were. With Toeyad's passing, however, she seemed to have become even more hateful, calculating, and manipulative.

Acutely aware of her husband's sudden annoyance, Lady Aron tried to soften the situation. She poured him a glass of sparkling peach wine, and with a somewhat self-effacing smile, handed it to him. "Look, my darling, it is no secret that I dislike Kandide, but the Frost must take precedence. One spoiled, arrogant princess cannot be allowed to threaten all of nature.

Even you know that."

"What can we—"

"I have it on good authority that our dear King Toeyad built a sanctuary for Imperfects somewhere. Tell me, my handsome husband, what do you know about a secret place somewhere in the Mists?"

Almost choking on his wine, Lord Aron simply stared at her.

THIRTY-THREE

The sun rose early the next morning, and with it, Kandide. She was anxious to leave. *After all,* she thought, *I'm not anything like them.* Curiously, the pains in her shoulder had ceased. *Maybe Leanne did help my wing a little,* she mused, looking in the mirror at its still bent and twisted shape. *Well, not enough. Anyway, I must be going.*

Outside her window, the early morning sky was just beginning to streak with vivid pink and amber colors. It would be a good day for traveling, as there were no rain clouds and the air was warm. *Hopefully, the weather will be this nice where I am going,* she thought. Remembering what Selena had told her about needing to be far enough inside the Mists—where the Veil starts to thin—in order to transport, Kandide began calculating the coordinates for her journey. Now that she knew exactly where she was, she could transport to anywhere.

Perhaps I should go to the meadows—maybe by the waterfall. There's an old abandoned mill house there. It'll provide shelter until I decide what to do. Or, I could go to the edge of the woods near the lowlands. I wonder if father's old cabin is still standing.

In any case, right now I need to find something to eat. With her cape pulled tightly around her shoulders, Kandide quietly tiptoed out of her bedroom and down the long hallway. Having stubbornly refused the meal that Selena sent up the night before, she was absolutely starving. *There must be something left over in the kitchen,* she thought. Perhaps she could even pack a basket to take on her journey. Since she still had no idea where she was going, or what she would find when she got there, a big basket would be nice!

Turning the corner to enter the kitchen, Kandide discovered that it was already bustling with activity. Had she not been so very hungry, she probably would have fled without stopping. The mouthwatering smell of hot, freshly baked biscuits, honey, jams, and fruit, however, was more than Kandide could resist. *Besides, what would a brief delay hurt? A good meal will give me strength. After all, I'll be on my own soon enough.*

"Why, good morning, Your Majesty," remarked a very surprised Margay. She was of the Air clan who tend the winds. She was also clearly missing both of her wings and looked more like a short rotund elf than a Fée. Nevertheless, she was obviously in charge of the kitchen, darting from place to place, with a jump here and a leap there. "My name is Margay. Selena tells me you liked my shortbread."

"Yes, very much," Kandide answered with a polite nod. "And thank you for the recipe. My chefs will put it to good use.

I was . . . uh, wondering if I might have a bite to eat."

"But of course." Margay hastily ordered a place set for Kandide at a long serving table. "Would you not, however, prefer to—?"

"This will do just fine," Kandide replied. "I . . . I'm afraid I am in a bit of a hurry."

"Well, well, look who's up early." Jake suddenly appeared in the doorway. "Nice of you to come down for breakfast . . . Kandide. You're welcome to eat in the dining hall, you know." Snatching a biscuit from the plate about to be served to her, he took a bite. "Mmm . . . Margay, these are even better than usual!"

"Now you stop that, Jake." She swatted at him. "In case you don't know who you are speaking to, this is Her Majesty Queen Kandide, and she's in a hurry."

"Well, then," turning to Kandide, Jake bowed. "I beg your pardon . . . Your Majesty." In a somewhat sarcastic gesture, he waved his hand in an exaggerated flourish.

Kandide barely acknowledged his words or actions. Instead, she turned her attention to Margay. "It's quite all right, Margay, I must be leaving now, anyway."

"Leaving?" Both of them queried at once.

"Yes. I . . . have other duties that require my immediate attention. I would be most appreciative, however, if you would pack a basket for me to take on my journey. The biscuits are truly wonderful and your jellies are some of the best I have ever tasted." Kandide almost swallowed an entire biscuit whole.

"Why, of course, Your Majesty. I shall notify Selena of your intended departure." Margay ordered one of her helpers to do so.

"I know she will want to see that you are safely along your way."

"That won't be necessary. I . . . uh, have already informed her." Kandide motioned to the basket as Margay filled it with hot biscuits, commenting, "Perhaps a few more and some fresh fruit would be nice."

"But, Your Majesty, I am sure Selena would wan—" Margay's tone was anything but sure.

"Just the basket will do." Kandide was polite, but regally firm.

"As you wish." She filled the basket to overflowing. Then, after covering it with a brightly colored gingham cloth, Margay curtsied and handed it to Kandide.

Nodding a courteous thank you, Kandide, with basket in hand, quickly departed.

"Well, I'll be!" Jake exclaimed. "How could a Fée as wonderful and caring as King Toeyad have raised such a daughter?"

"You knew her father?" Margay looked a bit surprised.

"Yep! Served right next to him in the after-wars. I was his First. Queen Tiyana and I are from the same clan."

"Wow!" piped up one of the younger Fée who was helping to prepare the breakfast. "You really knew King Toeyad?"

"Tell us about the clan wars, Jake," chimed in another.

"Now, Lindra," Jake answered, "I've told you that story a hundred times."

"Tell the rest of us." "Yeah, I haven't heard it!" "Please . . . please . . . please, Jake!" A chorus of voices rang out from the kitchen staff.

"Maybe later. I have a feeling I should tell Selena that her niece is leaving. I'm not so sure that she is aware of it."

THIRTY-FOUR

After leaving the protection of gated wall that surrounded the château, Kandide began carefully making her way into the Mists so she could transport. Vines clawed at her from every direction, and the ground was as black and slimy as when she arrived.

This should be far enough, she thought as she snapped a troublesome branch in two. *Now, where should I go? To the old mill house by the lake. I can stay there until I decide what to do.*

But before Kandide could gesture to transport, she heard an agonizing shriek. Startled, she instinctively ducked behind the closest tree.

Was it a shriek or a whine? Kandide wasn't sure. Something, however, sounded as though it was injured. No, she would not go and see. *It might be dangerous,* she rationalized. *I must think only of myself now.* Kandide started to gesture, once again, when she heard the same pitiful sound. Something, she did not know what, made her stop and look around for the source of the desperate cry. She hastily scanned the area. Suddenly, it came into view. She could only stare in disbelief. There, in a small clearing a short distance ahead, was a large white creature. It was a griffin—a real, live griffin! But what was it doing in the Mists?

Tangled in some sort of a snare, the poor creature was struggling desperately to free itself. The griffin's beautiful white-feathered neck was completely entangled in a thick rope, as were its hind legs. Barely able to move, the harder the poor creature struggled, the tighter the ropes became.

Cautiously, Kandide made her way toward the frenzied animal. "Don't worry, I'll help you," she whispered, in an attempt to calm it down. As she approached, however, the griffin began screeching at her, frantically clawing the air. She jumped back. "Hey, careful, take it easy. I won't hurt you."

Griffins were known for their fierce, elusive nature, so how this one could have been captured, she was not sure. They were also quite powerful, with the head, wings, and talons of an eagle, the body of a lion, and a tail that was forked like that of a mythical serpent.

"Who could have done this to you?" she again whispered as she inched a little closer to the helpless animal. Thankfully, it stopped clawing at her. She could see that the griffin's golden eyes were already beginning to glaze over from being so tightly restrained. Its white neck feathers were stained bright red where the ropes had cut into its flesh. In spite of being hopelessly trapped, it had a sense of pride that Kandide could instantly relate to. "You poor thing," she exclaimed, as she tried to assess the best way to release the snare. In doing so, however, Kandide discovered something else: not only was the griffin trapped, she was also very pregnant. "Take it easy, girl. I'll get you out of there; I promise."

The griffin began screeching and clawing again. This time, it was not at Kandide. From a nearby tree, a terrifyingly ghoulish beast leapt to the ground. Growling ferociously, it landed only a few meters away from where she was standing. With leathery, batlike wings, and large white fangs that dripped a gelatinous green drool, it was the ugliest creature Kandide had ever seen. Matted, patchy brown and black fur covered its long bony arms, and it had hands that ended in sharp, clawing fingers. Its beady red eyes focused directly on Kandide.

"A garglan?" she gasped, stunned to see such a beast.

A cross between a goblin and a gargoyle, garglans, like griffins, were thought to be extinct, except maybe as guards to the Banshee caves—*and that's only a rumor,* Kandide thought. This one, however, was certainly no rumor. But how did it get here? The Banshee caves were not even close to the Mists.

No longer concerned with the griffin, the garglan had found even more tantalizing prey. Fée are a special delicacy to these beasts. When devoured, their essence generates enough energy for the garglan to live on for weeks—sometimes even longer.

Not sure what to do, Kandide grabbed one of the biscuits from her basket and tossed it toward the beast. The creature caught it and, hissing with delight, greedily consumed the tasty treat.

"You like that, do you? Here, try this." She threw an apple off to the side, hoping to create a momentary distraction. Moving like a flash to catch it, the garglan instantly gobbled up the fruit as well. Drool dribbled down its chin. Its blood-red eyes darted back and forth between her and the basket.

"I have a basket full of treats. I'll give it to you if you go away." She tossed another biscuit. In all her life, Kandide had never faced real danger. Battle games with the Royal Guard were one thing, but a creature such as this was quite a different matter. She didn't even have a bow, or a sword, or anything. *Okay, keep calm, Kandide. Keep calm. What would Father do?* she asked herself.

As she stared at the dreadful beast, a second growling noise came from behind her. Her heart began to pound. Another, larger and even more hideous-looking garglan leapt out from behind a dead tree trunk. The griffin began screeching madly. Her large wings were flapping as she desperately tried to escape.

Before Kandide realized what was happening, the second garglan grabbed the basket from her hand. Hissing, it scurried up a tree with its prize. Howling in defiance, the first garglan darted up after it. The two began squabbling over the treats. Biscuits were flying everywhere.

Realizing that she had only moments to save herself, Kandide started to gesture to transport, but then abruptly stopped. She looked at the helpless griffin and knew that she could not leave it. Nor did she have the power to transport such a large creature. If only she could fly, she could release the snare from the tree branch where it was fastened. If only she had thought

GARGLAN

to bring a knife, she could cut it loose. If . . . if . . . if!

If only "if" could help! Kandide's hand slid into the pocket of her cape. She felt the feather her father had given her only days before. "Great! Why couldn't he have given me a knife?" she mumbled. Curiously, however, there was something odd about the way the feather felt. The silver band was hot, as though pulsing with some sort of energy. Suddenly, she spotted a glint of silver in the mossy undergrowth. A fruit knife must have fallen from the basket when the garglans scurried up the tree with it.

"It's not much, but . . ." Kandide picked it up. Incredibly, the energy from the feather seemed to flow right through her body and into the knife. The blade suddenly glowed white hot, as though it had been forged just that moment. The griffin was breathing heavily, and she knew it could not last much longer. Without hesitation, Kandide sliced through the first rope that constrained the exhausted animal. At least now its head was free.

Just as the rope was cut, however, the smaller garglan leapt from the tree. Its curiosity over the basket of treats obviously satisfied, it was now ready for a more substantial meal. Determined not to let it near the mother-to-be, Kandide turned to face the hideous beast. *If I do not survive,* she thought, *at least the griffin might still get away. Father would be proud.* Clutching the feather even tighter, Kandide felt its power continuing to surge through her body and into the knife. She slashed at the other restraint that was holding the griffin's feet, and it, too, quickly gave way.

"Go!" she shouted, not daring to take her eyes off the

garglan. "Hurry! You must get back to the château!"

Weighted down by the baby inside, and exhausted from its struggle to free itself, the majestic animal could barely move. It wasn't able to fly at all.

With her attention focused on the first garglan, Kandide did not see the larger one leap from the tree. It landed directly on top of her, and both she and the hideous beast dropped to the ground. Almost as if it was self-directed, the white-hot knife blade struck the creature's shoulder. Foul-smelling black ooze sprayed across Kandide's face and neck. The stench was nauseating. Shrieking, the stunned beast paused just long enough for her knife to strike again. This time, the blade slashed its throat. After another spray of thick, slimy black liquid, the garglan stopped moving. Its enormous dead weight fell on top of Kandide. With all her might, she shoved the creature aside.

Wiping the slime from her face, she shouted to the griffin, "Go! You must save your baby!"

As Kandide started to stand up, the other ghoulish fiend leapt at her. His sharp claws were aimed directly at her throat.

*"I don't think I repulse you.
I think you repulse you!"*

THIRTY-FIVE

Remarkably, the garglan's reach fell short by nearly a meter. Bewildered, Kandide noticed that an arrow had gone right through its neck. Gazing around to find the projectile's source, she caught a brief glimpse of a curious vivid red flash in a tree just a few meters away.

From the opposite direction, a voice called out, "Are you all right?"

Startled, Kandide abruptly turned to see Jake with bow in hand. She quickly stood up, straightening her dress. Despite being splattered with black slime, Kandide remarked in her most dignified fashion, "Thank you, Jake."

"You're welcome . . . Your Majesty. Here." He walked over and handed her his fresh linen handkerchief.

Kandide tried not to seem overly grateful, yet there was no question that she was extremely pleased to see him. She was also happy to get the foul, smelly stuff off her face and hands. "I was doing quite well, you know."

"Indeed, you were," Jake answered. A hint of a smile crossed his lips. Spotting the small knife lying on the ground, he picked it up and handed it to her. "And with just a simple fruit knife, too." Indeed, it was, once again, just a simple fruit knife.

"Did you see that bright red flash in the tree over there?" she asked, pointing in the direction where it occurred.

Before Jake could answer, the griffin let out a whimper. They both turned to look. A tiny baby wiggled its way out from underneath its mother. "Jake, look!" The griffin began licking her newborn cub to clean away the afterbirth.

"Are you okay, girl? Are you okay?" Kandide cautiously approached her. The appreciative new mother responded with a soft purring noise. Her beautiful golden eyes glistened with the gratitude she would forever hold for Kandide's bravery in saving their lives. Griffins are powerful, fiercely independent creatures, but they are also extremely intelligent and intensely loyal when given cause.

Knowing that she had made a new friend, Kandide gently stroked the soft white feathers on her head. "Your little cub is beautiful," she whispered. The mother griffin nuzzled her hand, purring even louder.

Suddenly remembering that her crumpled wing was exposed, Kandide froze. "I . . . I . . . must be going now." She turned and quickly walked over to her cape.

Picking it up off the ground, Jake placed the garment around Kandide's shoulders. "Please don't go." His beautiful green eyes relayed his genuine concern.

"You . . . You . . . You don't understand. I . . . I must . . ."

"Why?"

"You can't possibly understand." Kandide's tone was a blend of defensive denial.

"I can't understand? Understand what?" Refusing to accept her arrogance, Jake looked at her bent wing and remarked, "That you aren't as perfect as you would have us believe? That in fact, you are a crumplewing? There, I said it; you are a crumplewing—an Imperfect like me, and Selena, and Leanne, and all of the rest of us here."

"You may leave now."

"You didn't come to visit us, did you? You were sent away."

"I said you may leave now!" Kandide was practically screaming at him.

"No, I will not . . . leave now!" Jake shouted back, even louder. "Might I remind you that this is my land, not yours!"

"How dare you speak to me like that?"

"Why? You're not *our* queen! I doubt if you are even *their* queen!"

"You repulse me . . . all of you!" Only her misplaced anger hid how desperate she really felt.

"I don't think I repulse you. I think *you* repulse you!"

Shocked at his reply, Kandide was determined, more than ever, not to show weakness. "Look at me. Go ahead then, look at me, Jake." She lowered her cape, and turned to fully reveal her wing. "What do I have to live for? My life is over."

"Really? Well, I saved it, so you owe me."

"That's highly debatable!"

"Not by my book." Jake crossed his arms, planting his feet

firmly on the ground.

"I didn't ask for your help."

"It doesn't matter. Until you can repay me, you are in my debt."

"How dare you!"

"No, how dare you, Kandide!" Jake had just about enough of her self-centered behavior. "You, of all Fée, are sworn to obey the honor of the Codes. You are in my debt. And as payment, I demand that you help me take the griffin and her cub back to the château so we can care for them until they are strong again."

"I am quite sure that you can handle that task on your own." Kandide was flippant in her retort.

Shaking his head, Jake stared at her. "Fine. Then stay out here." He walked over and helped the griffin to stand up, muttering under his breath. "How could King Toeyad have raised such a daughter?" Looking back at Kandide, he added, "I release you from your debt." Carefully lifting the baby griffin into his arms, he started to head off.

"Wait!" Kandide hollered. "You aren't going to just leave me out here ... alone, are you?" After all that had just happened, she was not quite sure what to do.

"Yep!" he replied as he continued walking.

THIRTY-SIX

"**S**tay out here as long as you like, Your Majesty." Jake responded, without even a glance back at Kandide. "But I . . ."

Stopping, he turned around to look at her. "It's up to you, Kandide, but I'm headed back to the château. Come on, girl. Come on!" he called to the mother griffin. However, no matter how much he called, she refused to budge. She simply stood there looking back and forth between the two Fée.

"More garglans might come," Kandide protested.

"As you said, you're quite capable of handling them on your own. Here, take my sword." He tossed it to her. "I'm sure you know how to use it."

Catching it, Kandide commented, "I could have been eaten, you know." Whether from fright, or perhaps from being rejected, Kandide's attitude began to shift. She was also immensely touched by the fact that the mother griffin seemed torn between leaving her and going home with Jake.

"I doubt it. Garglans usually like something a little more . . . tender!" Gently stroking the newborn cub, Jake again called the mother griffin to follow, and again she refused to leave Kandide.

"I suppose you could use my help getting her home."

"I'll manage!" Jake called to the griffin once more, "Time to go, girl."

"Will they accept me . . . if I agree to return, I mean?" Kandide was beginning to realize that he might actually leave her out there.

"Accept you?" Jake looked at Kandide. "They'll probably give you a medal! You just fought two garglans and saved the life of the only pregnant griffin in over half a century. Why, you're . . . you're a hero!"

"I am, aren't I? I mean . . . I've never been a hero before. Do you really think they would . . . accept me, I mean?"

"I think it's more a question: Will you accept us?"

"Well, I . . ."

"I guess there's only one way to find out."

"Okay, I'll return with you." Kandide sounded as though she was doing Jake a favor. "If you promise not to reveal my secret." She glanced back at her crumpled wing.

"Nope! But I promise to let you reveal it first, as long as you don't take too long."

"Then I shall remain here!" Kandide crossed her arms, stubbornly planting her feet firmly on the ground. "Won't we, girl?" She looked at the griffin, who slowly turned and looked at Jake, almost as defiantly as Kandide.

THIRTY-SEVEN

"Now I have two of you against me," Jake shrugged, shaking his head. "Females!" Knowing that Kandide's pride was all she really had left, he walked back to her and gestured for her to sit on a fallen log. "Look . . . sit down, Your Majesty. Please?"

"Stop calling me that. You yourself said I am not queen."

"Title or not, you're every inch a queen. That no one can ever take away from you. Please, won't you sit down for a minute, Kandide? Let's talk."

The beginning of a smile crossed her lips as she joined him on the fallen log. For all of her poise, it could well have been a throne. The mother griffin walked over to her. Settling next to Kandide, she nuzzled her hand. Jake carefully placed the tiny cub by its mother.

"When I rode alongside your father, I was a Perfect, too. Then that terrible accident happened. Your father carried me back to camp in his own arms."

"You knew my father?"

"Very well. My parents introduced him to your mother. Your father told me of a vision he had, that one day he would have a beautiful daughter who would rule Calabiyau, and all Fée would live in harmony."

"It is my sister, Tara, who has fulfilled that destiny. She now rules Calabiyau, not I."

"And not all Fée, either. Some of us are still not allowed to live in harmony with the rest."

"But . . ." Kandide started to say something, and then stopped. She realized that she was no longer sure how she felt.

"When the healers told King Toeyad that my feet could not be fixed, he assured me that I could go back to the castle and would be cared for. I was far too proud and ashamed—kind of like you."

"I . . ."

"And like you, I wouldn't let anyone see me. Not even my own father and mother."

"Did Father send you away?"

"No, of course not. King Toeyad was true to his word. But I just couldn't imagine the humiliation of spending my life crawling around on my knees. As soon as my strength returned, I left the camp. I'm told that he was very upset and that he and my parents sent search parties out to find me. They almost did, once, but I hid. I just couldn't face having anyone see me like that, nor did I want to humiliate my parents that way."

"What did you do? Where . . . where did you go? How did you live?"

"Hey, one question at a time. What I did was to feel sorry for myself a lot. Kind of like you."

"I cert—" Kandide started to protest, but Jake kept talking.

"I survived by flying a lot. You can't stay airborne forever, though. So, I learned to walk on my knees. It's a lot harder than you think."

"I can imagine." She started to chuckle at the thought of Jake walking around on his knees.

"Avoiding the occasional garglan was even harder."

"What did you do?"

"I made a short bow and some arrows, and began practicing, since a sword isn't the easiest thing to use while kneeling."

"I guess not," Kandide interjected with another slight laugh. "Where did you live?" She glanced around at the dark, misty woods, cringing at the thought of actually trying to survive in this hostile environment. One night was enough for her.

"I built a small shelter in a rock cave, half beneath the ground."

"Out here?"

"You get used to it—sort of." He, too, looked around, shuddering as he remembered those awful years—the cold, the dampness, and mostly how very alone he felt. "One day, when I was sitting there, feeling particularly sorry for myself, I heard what sounded like a young child calling, so I started searching. That's when I found Leanne."

"Leanne?"

"Yeah, Leanne. When she was not more than five or six

years old, she was sent away because of losing her sight. When I found her, she could barely walk, she was so weak from hunger and exhaustion. I can't believe a garglan didn't find her first. Anyway, I picked her up and carried her into my hut. I'll tell you this: she's a fighter. Puts me to shame. She'd bump into things, tumble over, then just get right back up and keep walking. Her determination was amazing. Nothing seemed to bother her. And so optimistic—something I hadn't been in a lot of years."

"Optimistic, she is."

"After a while, I began to notice that she also had the Gift of Healing. Ironic, isn't it—that she can heal others, but not herself. Anyway, animals would bring their injured to her and she would make them well. One day, a wolf came and she healed its broken leg. We named him Trust because it took a lot of it to let Leanne help him. From then on, he was her constant companion."

"A wolf? What happened to him?"

"He gave his life protecting her from an attack by a couple of garglans when I was off gathering mushrooms—they're about the only thing that grows out here. Anyway, Trust killed the first garglan, almost immediately. But the second one jumped on his back and ripped open his throat. Even so, he wouldn't stop fighting. He died with the garglan's neck crushed between his jaws. Leanne was completely devastated, but there was nothing she could have done. It's the only time I've ever seen her truly depressed."

"I can imagine. I'm so sorry."

"Yeah, but Trust's offspring still live in the woods. Every

once in a while, when a new litter is born, they'll introduce the pups to us as if to say 'Protect these Fée, they are our friends.' There's been one watching us for quite some time now."

Kandide looked up. Giving a start, she saw a huge wolf lying not more than a few meters away.

"That's Ari. He leads the pack now." As Jake spoke, Ari walked over and nuzzled his hand. He cautiously sniffed at Kandide and the mother griffin.

"It's okay, boy, they're friends." The magnificent gray wolf wagged his flowing tail and barked a quick welcome, all of which the mother griffin totally ignored.

"I'm surprised that you didn't see him when you arrived," Jake continued. "He usually stands in the shadows and growls so new arrivals won't start heading in the wrong direction."

"That was Ari? He was at the cave I slept in before I found the Veil. I thought . . ." She reached over to pet the silvery wolf. "You were there to help me. Thank you, Ari."

"That he was. Although, if you didn't know, I can see how he could be a bit intimidating." Jake scratched the wolf's ears. "Good boy!" Another bark acknowledged Ari's concurrence.

"So then what happened?"

"He wanted a place that no one, including the High Council, could find or know about."

THIRTY-EIGHT

"**A**s Leanne grew older, her ability to heal became even stronger. So did her remarkable optimism. She just wouldn't let me feel sorry for myself. It was Leanne who suggested that I make a set of feet so that I could walk. At first, it was very frustrating. They kept falling off, or I would trip over myself." Jake stood up and began imitating his clumsiness.

Kandide started to giggle, encouraging him to pantomime even more, which he did. "I bet dancing was tough!"

"Oh, I don't know!" Reaching out, Jake pulled her up and began purposely tripping all over her feet, while singing a lively tune:

> *Step to the left, step to the right.*
> *The faeries are out and about tonight.*
> *Watch them dance, watch them whirl,*
> *Faster and faster the Fée can twirl.*
> *Step to the left, step to the right.*
> *The faeries are such a wondrous sight.*

"Where did you learn that song?" Kandide asked as they danced around the small clearing.

"From your father. I haven't thought of it for years." Jake continued to hum.

"Father used to sing it to me when I was a little girl. It's a human song." She began to sing along with him.

"Well, come on then. Pick up the pace a little. *Step to the left, step to the right . . .*" He began singing faster and faster.

"Hey, watch it!" she giggled, her toe having been the target of a misplaced boot.

Finally, dancing, singing, and laughing, the two of them tumbled over, landing on the wet ground.

"It's really good to see you laugh. You're even more beautiful when you do, you know," Jake whispered, extending his hand to help her up. His green eyes sparkled brighter than usual.

How could anyone be so handsome? she thought. For a brief second their eyes met. Realizing that she had totally lost her composure, Kandide snapped back into her protective mode. "Thank you. Uh . . . so . . . so then you met Selena?"

"Yep," he answered, motioning for her to sit back down on the log.

"Why did Father never tell me about the Veil, Jake?"

"Like Selena said, he wanted a place that no one, including the High Council, could find or know about—a secret place where *all* Fée can be safe and live in harmony with one another. Maybe he didn't think that you . . . well—"

"I understand." Kandide's tone reflected the fact that she truly did understand. "He was probably right."

"Anyway, Selena invited Leanne and me to join her. It really wasn't all that much back then, just a tiny cottage, but anything was better than living in a damp cave—or battling a garglan."

"You are right about that." She looked around, remembering what just happened. "So, what about your . . . your feet? They seem to work perfectly now . . . well, almost." Teasing him, she rubbed her own foot that he had stepped on.

"Sorry about that. Not long after we moved in, Trump came along. He's a Banshee."

"A Banshee?"

"Yeah, and a terrific jewelsmith. He lost an eye in a freak accident. So of course they—"

"Sent him away?"

"You got it."

"I've heard that the Banshees feed their Imperf—I mean . . . well, you know, to garglans." Now that she had actually seen the hideous beasts, Kandide shuddered at the thought.

"They do. Somehow, Trump was allowed to just leave. He never said why. We found him in the Mists clinging to an enormous bag of jewels. He was half-dead from his injuries. Said he'd been out there for days."

"So you just brought him into the château?"

"Well, we could hardly leave him there. Leanne healed him back to health."

Still dumbfounded at the thought of a Banshee living among the Fée, Kandide questioned, "Weren't you afraid he might kill someone? I mean, he is a Banshee."

"That he is. We try to judge everyone for who they are, not what they are, Kandide. I'll admit, however, it did take a while for him to be accepted. To his credit, Trump knew he would have to earn our trust and respect, and he worked twice as hard as anyone to get it."

"So you trust him?"

"I do. It was Trump who helped me fashion feet that work almost like real ones. He took some of his diamonds and made them round to act as joints for my ankles and toes, and then carved the feet out of hardened wood. See?" Jake pulled off his boots to show the sparkling diamond joints. "Selena made the straps that hold them on. And look! They're almost as good as new." He did a little jig in his bare wooden feet.

"That's amazing."

"We're working on wings now." Jake continued talking as he slipped his boots back on.

"So you said."

"Yeah, except we just can't seem to get them to work right."

"Why not?"

"I'll show you when we get back, but we had better get going." Realizing that they had been gone for quite some time, Jake stood up to leave. "As you well know, it's not very safe out here. A garglan can smell death for miles, and we don't need any more of them to find us."

"What about these?" She pointed to the two creatures lying in pools of black slime.

"One of their buddies will find them soon enough. I hear tell they eat their own dead. Even vultures won't touch a dead garglan."

Kandide cringed at the thought. "I can't say I blame them."

Jake gave Ari a pat on the head, telling him to be extra careful.

Briefly hesitating, Kandide looked for one last bit of reassurance. "Are you sure they will accept me, Jake?"

"Probably . . . I mean, I have," he teased with a bit of a smile as he extended his hand to help her up. He then picked up the baby griffin. "Come on, let's go find out who accepts whom."

With the mother griffin following closely at Kandide's side, the four of them set off toward the château.

"You know full well that we simply cannot let the Frost go beyond that date."

THIRTY-NINE

As Tara told the Council of her decision to send Teren in search of Kandide, protests could be heard from every corner of the room. "We cannot let him go, at least not alone," Lord Socrat insisted.

"You won't even tell us where he intends to search," added a very concerned Lady Alicia.

"I think it's a good idea to let him go," Lord Aron hastily interjected. Still not sure if he should have told his wife anything about the Mists, he was greatly relieved to learn that Teren, not his wife, would be the one to conduct the search.

"I agree, my dear," Lady Aron chimed in with a caustic grin. "Let him have until the Winter Solstice."

"But that's in three days!" Tara exclaimed.

"Yes. And if your brother does not return within that time, then I am afraid the only choice is for Tiyana to deploy the small portion of the Gift that Toeyad gave her."

"But that's not nearly enough time," Teren protested.

"Take it or not; the decision is yours." Lady Aron was unyielding. "You know full well that we simply cannot let the Frost go beyond that date. It is already becoming most perilous."

"Then I'll be back in three days," Teren hastily agreed, not wanting to push his luck with the other Council members. "Mother, Tara, can you help me get ready?" The determined young prince was looking for any excuse to hustle them out of the chamber before the rest of the Council had the chance to object.

"Good idea," Tara nodded. "Shall we, Mother?"

Hesitating, it was Tiyana who started to protest, "I ask you to reconsider, and—"

Lady Aron was quick to cut her off. "Teren has made his request, Tiyana, and the Council has approved it." She looked at the other Council members for any sign of disagreement. None spoke up. "It is his choice to go or not. Something must be done. At least your son realizes that much."

"She is right, Tiyana," Lord Salitar interjected, trying to soften Lady Aron's words. "If we do not see the Frost by the Winter Solstice, the consequences will surely be irreversible."

"And if we do not see you, Prince Teren, on the eve of the third day," Lady Aron quickly added, "then Tiyana, do you agree to use your portion of the Gift to change the seasons?"

Glaring at her, Tiyana's answer was without emotion.

"As you have stated, Lady Aron, it will be my only choice."

"Don't worry, Mother, I'll be back!" Teren looked first at his mother and then over to Lady Aron; his expression changed to a scowl.

Her response was a mocking smile. "So we all . . . hope."

Teren, Tara, and their mother left the Council, and headed toward Tiyana's private chamber.

Lady Aron also hastily departed.

*"Now, were you able to appropriate
the additional garglans?"*

FORTY

Reappearing just outside the Royal Guard's quarters, Lady Aron approached Asgart, who was just getting off duty. Looking at his new uniform, she commented, "Stripes suit you, Captain—I believe that is your title now."

"Thank you, my lady. Uh . . . could we talk over there?" He motioned for her to follow him to a well-hidden area near a side garden.

"So, do you like your new rank?" she questioned, casually strolling beside him.

"Very much. It is strange, though, Captain Erley becoming sick like that—and so suddenly. I hope he recovers soon. He taught me a great deal when I served under him."

"I am sure he will recover . . . eventually. Now, were you able to appropriate the additional garglans? I'm in a hurry."

"Begging your pardon, My Lady, garglans don't just grow on trees, you know." Asgart kept his voice very low. "It was hard enough getting the first two for you. What happened to them, anyway? I didn't see them at your villa, and why do you want so many more?"

"Questions. Questions. Questions. My dear Asgart, when are you going to learn that I do the asking? Let's just say that I will sleep better knowing there are a lot more of them on the job—so to speak. Now, did you get them or not?"

"There are fifteen more chained outside your summer villa. You have no idea what I had to do to get them. If the Banshees ever find out that it was—"

"You've done very well, Captain. Once again, I shall see to it that you are handsomely rewarded. I understand that Lady Socrat is in need of a new lady-in-waiting. Perhaps your wife might be interested?"

Without waiting for his answer, Lady Aron vanished.

FORTY-ONE

Seeing Jake and Kandide entering the Great Hall, Selena rushed up to them. "Thank the earthly spirits that you are both safe."

"Thank Kandide. She saved the griffin and her newborn cub from sure death by a couple of garglans." Jake carefully handed the tiny creature to Selena. Its mother softly growled, nuzzling Kandide.

"Well, what have we here? The first griffin cub to be born in over half a century." Selena was elated. "You must tell me what happened. Oh dear, you both do look a fright."

As Kandide and Jake relayed their story, the entire room filled with Fée of every sort to listen. When Jake told how Kandide killed the first garglan with "just a simple fruit knife," they began to applaud and yell, "Queen Kandide! Queen Kandide! Queen Kandide!"

"Perhaps you'd better say something," Selena urged her niece.

Kandide silenced the crowd. "Thank you, but I did have a little help." She felt the feather safely inside her pocket, and then quickly smiled at Jake. "There is something else you must know," she continued. "I . . . I am not queen."

A confused hush fell over the crowd, which by now was overflowing the large room.

"I am, uh . . . I was sent a—" Pulling her cloak tightly around her shoulders to conceal her crumpled wing, she blurted out, "Jake, I simply can't!" She then rushed out of the room.

The griffin, who had been lying in the hallway with her cub, stood up. Spreading her massive wings, she blocked Kandide from passing. The new mother emitted a low growl and gently pushed her tiny baby forward. Picking him up, Kandide sat down on a long bench and fondly cuddled the little cub.

Jake rushed over to her. "Listen to them, Kandide. Do you think they care if you have a crumpled wing?"

"I care!" Standing up, Kandide started to hand the baby griffin to Jake. Before she could do so, his mother growled again, pushing Kandide back down on the bench.

"Looks like Gertie doesn't want you to leave, either," Jake smiled.

"Gertie? Is that her name?"

"Yep, Gertie Griffin."

"That's a silly name."

Gertie glared at Kandide, and then let out another deep-throated growl.

"Oh, sorry, Gertie. It's a lovely name. Really!" Kandide

smiled rather sheepishly. Looking at Jake, she sighed, "It's no use. I am just not—"

"Well, get over it, or . . . or Gertie and I will personally take you back out there and feed you to the garglans. And I was just kidding, they'll eat anything, tender or not!"

The mother griffin nodded in agreement.

"How dare you speak to me that way—and you, too!" Kandide looked at Jake, then Gertie, trying not to smile. In an attempt to change the subject, she added, "You know, her little cub needs a name as well."

"How about Courage, in honor of his savior—and because that is what is needed right now?" Jake looked at Gertie, who shook her head up and down in agreement.

"Well, if Gertie agrees, who am I to argue? Courage it shall be." Kandide petted the tiny creature, who purred with delight while rubbing its head on her arm.

"That's the Kandide I know." Jake reached out to tilt her chin up. "Now, get back in there and act like the queen your father raised you to be. Something about 'strength and courage,' he always used to tell me."

Kandide couldn't help but smile at the fact that Jake knew her father's words. "But what can I do if I stay here? I have no healing gift. I can't carve or sew. I don't even know how to cook or—"

"No, I don't suppose you do. But you are a very brave queen, and that's pretty special. I suggest you go back in there and . . . and . . . well, why not be a queen?"

Carefully setting the baby griffin down next to Gertie, and with all of the self-confidence that she could muster, Kandide walked back into the Great Hall. Silencing the cheering crowd, she stated, "My sister, Tara, is Calabiyau's queen now. I . . . I was sent away." Letting her cape drop, Kandide, at last, exposed her injured wing. To her surprise, there was no reaction. No one jeered or hissed. They all just sat there eagerly listening to what she had to say. "But if I may be of some help here," she looked over at Jake and then toward Selena for more reassurance, "and if you will have me, I would like to stay."

Again, cheers broke out. Everyone stood up, applauding.

One young Fée hollered, "Will you be our queen? We don't have one. I mean . . . will you consider it, Your Majesty?"

Kandide's eyes filled with tears. Never had anyone appreciated her just for herself. With true humility, perhaps for the first time in her life, she responded with a deep curtsy. "It will be my honor to serve you all."

The crowd was ecstatic. Selena finally quieted everyone down. "I suggest we prepare a feast to honor Her Majesty—the Veil's first queen."

Again, cheers rang out. Courage leapt into Kandide's arms. The tiny cub nuzzled her face; his golden eyes sparkled with joy. Even Gertie let out an approving howl as she pushed her way through the crowd to sit proudly at Kandide's side.

At peace for the first time since the accident, Kandide thought to herself, *Perhaps I have found my true home. Perhaps the fates have decreed this to be my destiny.*

FORTY-TWO

Are you sure that you have everything?" Tiyana asked. She, Teren, and Tara were in her private chamber.

"Yes, Mother," Teren replied for at least the tenth time. "You worry way too much."

"My child, as far as I know, your father and I are the only ones who have ever returned from the Mists. For fear of the Veil being discovered, we stopped going there not long after Toeyad created it. There could be immense danger." Tiyana's voice contained a great deal of uncertainty and concern.

"I have to do this, Mother," Teren argued. "I won't let you risk your life deploying the Gift."

"Maybe you should take guards," she urged.

"He can't," Tara insisted. "You said yourself that no one else must know about the Veil. Besides, Kandi might think that she is being forced by the Council to return. Then she'll never come back. You know how she is."

Nodding her head, Tiyana sighed, bidding Teren one last request: "Be extremely wary, my son. Take your father's sword and use this talisman if you are in any danger." She placed a small glowing orb, suspended from a golden chain, around his neck. "Should you need help, rub it three times clockwise, and I will be able to find you." Tiyana strapped Toeyad's sword around his waist and then hugged her son.

"I'll be fine, Mother, don't worry." He hugged her back. "I love you."

"I love you too, my son." Tiyana's face revealed her anguish.

"He'll be fine, Mother. You'll see." Tara squeezed her mother's hand.

"Remember, Teren, even transporting, the journey will take you several hours. The Mists are quite far. May the earthly spirits protect you." Tiyana gestured, and Teren vanished in a glimmer of light.

"I . . . uh . . . guess I should get back to the Council. Who knows what they are up to?" Tara also gestured, instantly vanishing from her mother's side.

FORTY-THREE

"So, what do you think?" Jake showed Kandide a set of perfectly formed wings. They were in a large workroom off to the side of the château where Jake was experimenting with different types of mechanical extremities, including arms, hands, and legs.

"I think they are quite preposterous," she responded. "The shape is correct, but the wings are far too heavy. How did you make them?"

"The spiders spin their silk in the shape we need. But it isn't durable enough by itself," he answered.

"So we tried dipping them in oak resin," interjected Egan, the young, wingless Fée for whom the wings were being created. "That's what makes them so heavy."

"Next we tried a sugar solution," Jake continued to explain.

"Sugar?" Kandide questioned.

"Yeah, and it was perfect, at least until it got wet. Poor Egan landed right in the lake." Jake started chuckling as he relayed how funny it looked to see Egan's wings melt away, leaving him thrashing about in the water.

"That's terrible," Kandide scolded. Even she, however, had to cover her mouth so as not to giggle at the thought of his wings melting.

"It wasn't funny!" Egan protested, finding no humor at all in their discussion. "I could have drowned, you know!"

Born without wings, Egan had lived in the Mists since he was a baby. He was still quite young, no more than six in human years. And with his slightly turned-up nose, big blue eyes, honey-colored hair, and mischievous smile, he was truly adorable. He knew little more of his parents than which clans they belonged to, but that didn't stop him from taking pride in his heritage.

"Egan is of the Earth and Fire clans, and water is definitely not his favorite thing," Jake continued. "He even avoids stepping across puddles. And since he can't fly, he's been known to walk for hours to avoid crossing the lake—even in a boat."

"My mother's clan doesn't swim," Egan insisted. "Fire and water don't go together, you know."

"Well, in that case, we really do need to solve this problem," Kandide insisted with a nod. "I have an idea. There is a very, very old finish called shellac. It is light, can be thinned, dries hard, and won't melt when it gets wet."

"But it's made from little beetles." Egan was aghast at the thought.

"That's right," Kandide nodded.

"My father's clan protects them. They eat the dead trees to make the soil better. I could never kill a beetle just so I can fly," Egan exclaimed.

Jake hastily interjected, "We respect all life here, Kandide. No matter how small or seemingly insignificant."

"You are more like my father than you know. He, too, would allow no creature to be sacrificed for his convenience." Turning to Egan, she added, "Then we shall just have to find another solution. Tell me, how do you make the prototype wings flap?"

"Well, that's another thing we had to solve. It's not perfect, but Egan moves his shoulder muscles back and forth, not unlike real wings. Show her, Egan."

The young Fée imitated the motion.

"He can't fly as far as with normal wings, but at least he won't have to walk around the lake," Jake teased.

"What would happen if you mixed sugar with a thinly diluted solution of oak resin? The sugar will provide the stiffness, and the diluted resin might just be enough to seal it," Kandide suggested.

"Hey, you know, that just might work. What do you think, Egan?"

"It might. Can you ask the spiders to spin new ones so we can try it? Can you, Jake? Can you?" Egan was excited about Kandide's suggestion.

"You bet."

"Good, and while they are doing that, I am going to teach Egan to swim." Kandide looked straight at Egan and smiled.

"No, you're not! I'm not going anywhere near that lake again!" Egan started to run away.

Kandide reached for his hand to stop him from leaving. "Grab his other hand, Jake. Egan is going to get a swimming lesson."

"Let me go! Let me go!" Egan protested, dangling between the two of them as they headed off toward the lake.

FORTY-FOUR

Finding a quiet spot on a large rock near the edge of the water, Jake and Kandide finally released the squirming young Fée. Not, however, before Kandide evoked a promise from him not to run off.

"You won't throw me in?" he cautiously confirmed before agreeing to stay.

"No, Egan," she promised. "We won't." Kandide looked over at Jake, and then motioned toward the water, "Shall we?"

"Dressed like that?" He gestured to her clothes. "Allow me." With a flick of his wrist, both she and Jake were instantly wearing bathing costumes.

"How did you do that?" Kandide was amazed.

"A little trick Trump taught me. Those Banshees are pretty clever."

"You'll have to teach it to me."

"You'll have to catch me first." Jake dove into the water from the large rock where they were sitting. Kandide quickly followed. The lake was cool and crystal clear, having been fed from the mountain springs. Together, they swam to a tiny island not far from the shore, where Kandide immediately started a water fight.

"Follow me," Jake called, before diving underwater to avoid a carefully aimed splash. He led her through a spectacular underwater tunnel filled with freshwater coral, beautifully colored fish, and graceful plant life. The two effortlessly swam through it to the opening on the other side. There, surrounded by steep, towering red rock cliffs, was a natural limestone pool with steaming hot water.

"What is this place?" Kandide wondered, looking around. She had never seen anywhere quite like it before.

"It's a hot spring that's heated from underwater volcanic activity. It's very therapeutic."

"The heat does feel good on my wing. It still aches sometimes."

"I'm sure it must. But I've never heard you complain."

"Well, you will if you don't bring me back here again—and soon! It's so beautiful."

"Almost as beautiful as you, Kandide." Jake's eyes sparkled in the reflected sunlight of the pool as he stared into her equally beautiful eyes. He reached out to touch her cheek and her whole body tingled. But as he leaned closer to kiss her, she demurely turned away.

"I've never been ... to a place like this before," she smiled. Not wanting her true feelings for him to show, Kandide hastened to add, "We shouldn't . . . leave Egan alone for too long, you know." With a broad grin, she slapped her hand on the water, splashing Jake squarely in the face. He started to return the deed, but Kandide quickly dove beneath the surface. Coming up for air just in front of the underwater tunnel, she called, "I bet I can beat you back!"

"Think so? You're on!" The two of them began to race. Back through the tunnel and around the island they went. While Jake could easily have beaten Kandide, chivalry dictated that he let her win—not, however, by very much.

"You didn't even try," she called out, arriving at the shore just a few strokes ahead.

"Oh, yes I did," he grinned. "You just . . . swam way too fast! Why, Kandide, is that a blush I see?" he teased, taking her hand and gently kissing it.

"Don't be silly!" Kandide abruptly turned her attention to Egan. "Come on in," she beckoned, splashing him with water as well.

"I don't think so." Egan shook his head, darting to avoid the spray.

"Oh, come on. Just think, you could be the first in either of your clans to learn to swim," Kandide responded, encouraging him to think about it.

"I could?"

"I think so," Jake nodded.

"Do . . . do you think I really can?" Egan was not at all sure about learning to swim, but the thought of being the first to do anything definitely appealed to him.

"Why not?" Jake replied. "Come on, we'll hold on to you."

With a flick of Jake's wrist, Egan also found himself in a bathing costume. "You're already dressed for it."

"O . . . okay. I mean . . . maybe." Egan cautiously approached the edge of the lake. With a great deal more coaxing, he finally put one toe in the water, and then just as quickly pulled it out. "It's so . . . so . . . wet," he objected.

"It certainly is," Kandide agreed, encouraging him even more. "That's why it's called water. Come, take my hand, I won't let you drown."

Slowly, very slowly, Egan tiptoed into the water, hesitating at every step.

"It's okay, Egan, we have you." Jake also held on to him. "Now lean forward and just relax. Keep your head up. See, you're already floating."

"I am!"

FORTY-FIVE

Materializing in the middle of the dense, misty forest, Teren was not at all sure which way to turn. Gnarled, tangled vines covered almost every inch of open space. The dead tree branches were so thick they shut out most of the sunlight. Trying to compose himself and gather his courage, he cautiously looked around.

"Mother didn't tell me it was going to be this creepy," he thought aloud. "I wonder which way I'm supposed to go now." Taking a step forward, he slipped, landing flat on his bottom in the soggy under-marsh.

"I'm not sure, but I think you'd better get up!"

Teren whirled around. There, standing behind him, was his sister. "Tara! What are you doing here?"

"You didn't think I was going to let you have all the fun, did you?"

"Yeah, well you're not going to think it's fun when Mom finds out. How'd you follow me, anyway?"

"Hey, I know a few tricks myself, you know." Tara held out her hand to help him up. "Are you all right?"

Standing, he brushed himself off. "Yeah, but you won't be when we get back. Mom's going to kill you!"

"She may not have to. Look!" Tara pointed toward a hideous black form. Its beady red eyes were staring straight at her.

"Wha—what is it?" Teren stammered.

"A garglan, I think." Closer and closer the creature approached; its shrill hisses were terrifying. "I think we'd better go!"

"Where to?" Teren started to gesture.

"I'm not sure. This is exactly where Mother's coordinates sent us. It must be here . . . somewhere." Tara anxiously looked around.

"We can't just transport to somewhere. Where do you want to go?"

"Let me think, okay?" In fact, Tara had no idea where they should go.

"Well, while you figure it out, I think I can stop that thing. At least, I hope!" Teren mumbled a few magical words, then dramatically waved his hand, pointing his finger directly at the beast. Instantly, the garglan froze. "I did it! Hey, Tara, I did it!"

"Can you handle another one?" Tara asked, seeing a second garglan leap out from behind an old log. It was also madly hissing.

"Sure I can . . . I think!" He turned to point at the second garglan. But as he did, his finger left the first beast, and it shook free of the spell, hissing even louder.

"Uh . . . Teren, I think you—"

"Oops!"

"Oops?" Tara mimicked him as she grabbed his other hand and aimed it back at the first garglan. "What do you mean 'Oops'? Can you do this or not?"

"I've only tried it once on Kandide, and that was a game."

"Well, little brother, this is no game!"

Standing with his arms spread and fingers pointing, one at each garglan, he stammered, "I . . . I can do it! Really I can!"

"Then you'd better find some more fingers. Look over there!" Another garglan leapt onto the scene. Hissing and snarling, its bright pink tongue was dangling out of one side of its mouth and slimy drool was dripping down the other side. As soon as it appeared, so did another, and then another.

Spreading his fingers so that they pointed at each garglan, and muttering spells as fast as he could, Teren gasped for air. He was almost out of breath. "Okay, but after ten, you're on your own!"

"Give me your sword."

"Here . . ." He started to drop his hand to give it to her.

"Stop! Don't move!" Teren's arm flew back up—his fingers spread toward the four garglans on his right. "What are you doing?" Tara shouted. "You keep pointing. I'll get the sword."

Trying to keep his fingers aimed at all of the garglans at once, which had increased by at least another five, Teren was mumbling spells as fast as he could. "Oh great!" he hoarsely whispered. "I thi— thi— think you'd better decide where we should transport to—and quick. Look!" He motioned with the only thing he had left, his head.

Before Tara could turn to look, a huge wolf leapt from the

trees, landing directly in front of her.

"Ni— ni— nice boy," she stammered, cautiously holding out her hand for the wolf to sniff. Tara had healed wolves before, in the forest near her home. This place, however, was quite a different matter, and she had never seen a wolf so large.

Snarling and growling, the wolf turned and lunged, not at her, but at the garglans. From deep within its throat came a loud, ferocious howl. Several more wolves appeared. With fangs bared, they also began to snap and snarl at the beasts in an attempt to keep the "unfrozen" ones from coming any closer.

"What do we do now?" Teren asked.

"Just keep your fingers pointed—and don't stop mumbling that spell. I think the wolves are our friends."

"I think we could use some right about now. My arms are getting awfully tired."

"Yeah, well, they're going to have a long time to rest if you don't keep pointing." With sword in hand, and the wolves guarding her, she slashed at one of the frozen beasts' throats. "Take that!" she hollered, slicing through his neck.

"Oh, yuck!" Teren winced, as smelly black bile sprayed out from the creature. "I think I'm going to be sick."

"Well, before you do . . ." Tara whirled around, just in time to see another garglan start to leap at one of the wolves. "Over there!"

"Got it!" He mumbled the spell again. "But remember, I'm back up to ten again."

"Just keep pointing."

"Just keep slashing."

FORTY-SIX

Inside the château, Jake heard the ferocious howls from the wolves. He nearly dropped the sugar bowl that he had been holding to mix with the diluted tree resin. "That's Ari!" he exclaimed. "Tori, Benji," he hollered, "come with me. Grab your bows." Jake instantly flew out of the kitchen. His two companions were close behind.

"If only the vines weren't so thick, we could see better," Tori remarked as they sailed above the branches.

"Over there!" Benji pointed off to the left. "The garglans have them surrounded."

"Looks like the wolves are holding them off," Tori replied.

"Yeah, but I don't know for how long," Benji added. "Who's that with them?"

"Guess we'll find out. Release arrows on my command," Jake ordered. "And make them count. I don't know what is going on, but I've never seen so many garglans at one time."

Flying closer, he issued the command, "Ready ... fire at will!"

Flurries of arrows began flying through the air. The garglans shrieked in horror as the deadly shafts easily struck their intended marks. One by one they fell. Black ooze was dripping from the last remaining beast as it screeched, and then ran off in a fit of madness with an arrow piercing its shoulder.

Jake and his two companions landed in the center of the curious menagerie. The stench was horrific, but Tara, Teren, and all of the wolves were safe. Ari pranced over and licked Jake's hand to thank him.

"Good job, ole boy. Thanks!" Jake rubbed the wolf's head, and then petted and thanked each of Ari's companions. Turning to Tara, he introduced himself,. "Hello, I'm Jake. This is Tori and Benji."

"And I'm very grateful," Tara responded.

"Well, welcome, Very Grateful," Jake quipped as he looked her over, trying to determine why she could possibly be there.

"I'm Teren," her brother piped in.

"Hello, Teren. I think it's safe to drop your arms now." Jake motioned for him to do so.

"Oh! Yeah!" Teren began rubbing his wrists.

"Have you and Very Grateful come to join us in the Mists?" Jake inquired.

"My name is Tara," she replied, smiling, but with an under-tone of impatience.

"Tara? Her Majesty Queen Tara?" Jake and the other two quickly bowed.

"Yes, and this is my brother, Prince Teren. We've come to find our sister, Princess Kandide. Have you seen her? Do you know her, or where she might be?"

"Kan . . . Kandide?" Jake hesitantly asked. "What . . . what do you want with her?"

"You know her? That's great! Is she . . . is she okay?" Teren was eager for any sort of news.

"She's fine. What do you want with her, if I might ask, Your Majesty?"

"She holds the Gift of the Frost. And until she deploys it, the seasons cannot change."

"I thought it was unseasonably warm." Jake rubbed his neck. "Kandide has the Gift? Of course, from your father."

"Yes, and we must convince her to come back with us," Teren exclaimed.

Looking very concerned, Jake swallowed hard, then asked, "Come back?"

"She must return to the castle, or our mother may die. Please, if you know where she is, take us to her, immediately." Her tone was polite, but Tara's lack of patience was beginning to show.

"Tiyana may die? I'm confused?"

"I'll explain on the way. Please, Jake, you must take us to Kandide." Tara was insistent.

"Of course, but I request that you let me speak to her first, Your Majesty," Jake replied.

"As you wish," she nodded. "Now please, let's be off. We only have three days, and I'm afraid that getting Kandi to return may not be all that easy."

Once again, Jake turned to thank Ari and the other wolves. Then the five of them headed toward the château.

"So how did you follow me?" Teren asked as they soared above the gnarled treetops.

FORTY-SEVEN

"I was holding Mother's hand when she transported you, and instantly traced the coordinates," Tara explained.

"Where'd you learn that?"

"Maybe you should try actually reading some of those books."

"Now wait a minu—Wow!" Teren exclaimed, landing in the courtyard. He stared up at the spectacular château. "This is nothing like what Mother described!"

"Selena?" Tara questioned, seeing her mother's twin standing near the massive front doors of the palace.

"Yes . . . Tara? Teren? Can it really be you? I can't believe you are here—both of you? Are you all right?" Selena looked them up and down. They certainly didn't appear to be injured in any way. They were splattered with black slime, but not hurt or permanently injured.

"We're fine. Mother told us all about the Veil." Tara rushed over to her aunt, hugging her with joy.

"Yeah, but she didn't say it would be anything like this," Teren added, also hugging his aunt. "We need to see Kandide."

"Of course. I'm sure she'll be excited to see you. Please come inside." Selena motioned for them to do so. "My, how grown-up you both are. And you, Teren, your smile is exactly like your father's. You must tell me what is happening in Calabiyau. First Kandide appears, and now the two of you!"

"That's why we're here; we need to talk to Kandide," Tara persisted.

"I'll go fetch her while you two explain what's happening." Jake headed off as Selena escorted Teren and Tara to the Great Hall.

"Is everything okay out there, Jake?" Kandide queried. She and Egan were still in the kitchen, where they were carefully spraying the newly created sugar and resin solution onto his new wings.

"Well, sort of. Your sister and brother are here."

"What? Tara and Teren are here?"

"Yes. They want you to return home with them."

"What do you mean they want me to return home with them? Absolutely not! This is my home now, Jake." She looked at Egan, who nodded in agreement.

"Kandide, it's import—"

"So is the work we do here."

"You must at least see them," interjected Selena, who had just entered the kitchen. "From what they tell me, it is vitally important."

Kandide looked at Selena and then back at Jake. "Well, of course, I want to see them. What I meant was, I will not be leaving." Her tone was emphatic. "How did they find me, anyway?"

"Tiyana sent them," Selena answered.

"Mother sent them? Why? Are they okay? I must—"

"They are both fine," Selena assured her. "Come, they're very anxious to see you."

Kandide hurried out of the kitchen and down the hallway to meet her brother and sister. Although in her heart she knew they had come for the Gift, she could not help but be excited to see them. "Teren, Tara . . . I mean, Your Majesty, it's wonderful to see you." A broad smile crossed her face. Noticing how disheveled they looked, she commented, "I see you've met some of our gatekeepers."

"Yeah, we took care of them, though," Teren smugly replied.

"Especially after Ari and his friends showed up," Tara chimed in. "Oh, Kandi, we've missed you so." She hugged her sister. "You should be queen, not me."

"No, the crown of Calabiyau is yours. The Veil is my home now. I am its queen."

"That's wonderful, but did Jake tell you?" Tara insisted. "You must come back with us."

"You know I cannot go back. Besides, even if I could, I'm not sure I would. I'm loved and appreciated here for who I am, not just because I'm so beautiful . . . or perfect."

"Oh, Kandi, I love you too, and so does Mother, and so does Teren. We all love you, just the way you are."

"We appreciate you, too. We do. We all do!" Teren quickly added. "But Mother may pass if she tries to change the seasons."

"What?" Kandide had no idea what they were talking about. "What do you mean? Mother can't change the seasons. I'm the only one who can do that."

"She thinks she can—at least this once," Tara explained. "The Council will force her to use the small amount of the Gift that Father gave her, and that would take all of her strength."

"Kandide, Mother might die if she tries," Teren added.

"The Council can't force her to do that. Besides, Father didn't give her nearly enough of the Gift to trigger the Frost. Even Lady Aron must know that." Kandide's answer had a curious sense of indifference that surprised even Tara.

"Don't you care?" an equally surprised Teren pressed.

"Of course I care, Teren. It's just that . . . well, it was Mother who sent me away. I know she blames me for hastening Father's passing. And that she's ashamed of me now because of my wing."

"That is ridiculous and you know it!" Tara scolded. "Mother saved your life, Kandi. She sent you here to protect you. She knew Selena would take care of you."

"And that you'd be safe," Teren interjected, trying his best to reassure her. "How do you think we found you?"

"It was the only thing Mother could do," Tara insisted.

"She could have . . . she could have upheld my crowning. If Father were alive, he would never have let it happen."

"You know better than that, Kandi." Tara was furious. "Even Father could not have persuaded the High Council to let

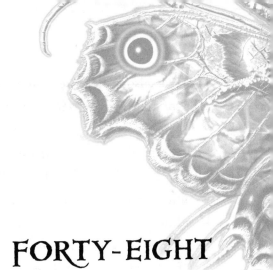

FORTY-EIGHT

Once Tara and Teren had cleaned up a bit, Kandide began showing her brother and sister around the château, introducing them to one Fée after another. She took a great deal of pride in showing off her new friends, and how remarkable it all was—the vineyards, the lake, the gardens, the beautiful artwork and tapestries—everything.

Next, Kandide introduced Tara and Teren to Leanne. "Leanne is a healer like you, Tara. She is helping to heal my wing. So far, we've had only a little bit of luck, but Leanne keeps trying. She's sure she can do it one day. Maybe if the two of you worked together?" she said, looking back and forth at the two healers.

"It is an honor to meet you, Your Majesty," Leanne replied with a curtsy.

"You are very kind." Tara nodded to acknowledge Leanne.

"It is also a pleasure to meet you, Prince Teren. Your sister tells me that you are quite the magi."

"She did?" Teren was delighted at the thought of his sister saying anything nice about him.

"Yes, she did. Tara, Selena tells me that your healing talent is quite strong. Perhaps we can channel together to help Kandide's wing. With several treatments, I am sure we can make an enormous difference."

"I would certainly love to try," Tara responded. "First, however, we must convince my sister to return home to deploy the Frost. Kandi?"

"The Frost? No wonder it is so warm for this time of the year," Leanne remarked. "You must seriously consider returning, Kandide. It's quite late in the season already."

Wanting to avoid answering, Kandide changed the subject. "Leanne is blind, yet it doesn't stop her from doing exactly what she wants. Does it, Leanne?"

"I do my best," she responded, and then turned to Tara. "Nothing much stops your sister, either."

"You got that right," Teren agreed.

"Did you know that she killed two garglans and saved Gertie and her newborn cub?"

"Is that so?" he replied. "Well, Tara and I kill—" Before he could finish his sentence, Tara kicked him. "Ouch! What did you do that for?" He rubbed his ankle.

"Oh, I'm sorry, Teren. My foot must have slipped." She glared at her brother.

Completely ignoring them, Kandide continued, "It was only one garglan. Jake killed the other, and Gertie is a griffin.

Her cub was the first to be born in over half a century." Even though Kandide tried to be modest, she just couldn't help herself. "They say I'm a hero. I guess I am."

"Well, I'm impressed! Aren't you, Teren?" Tara kicked him again.

"Uh . . . yeah. A hero!" he glibly answered. "Wow! One garglan, that's really impressive, Kandide."

"I had no idea there were any griffins left," Tara quickly added.

"Thanks to Kandide, there is now one more," Leanne responded with a smile.

"Leanne is also a hero," Kandide asserted. "She's helped virtually all of the Fée who live here. And she's a true inspiration, too. Nothing ever gets her down. Would you like to go to the lake with us, Leanne?"

"That is very kind of you, Kandide, but I have several more Fée to attend to before dinner. There seems to be a terrible outbreak of scraped elbows today."

"Then we'll see you later." Grabbing Tara and Teren's hands, Kandide whisked the two of them away. "If we hurry, we can watch the sunset over the water."

As they were leaving, Tara called back to Leanne, "Perhaps we can chat more over dinner?"

"That would be lovely, Your Majesty."

"Dinner, now that sounds like a good idea." Teren abruptly stopped. "I think we missed lunch. Come to think of it, we almost were lunch!" he chuckled.

"Don't remind me." Tara looked at him and shook her head.

"So, when do we eat, Kandide? I'm really hungry all of a sudden!"

"Later, Teren. First the lake." Kandide motioned for him to follow. "Come on."

Sitting on a large rock, overlooking the water, Tara gazed across the countryside. "It's really beautiful here. I see why you love it so very much."

"And I've learned a great deal as well," Kandide responded. "You know the expression 'beauty is only skin deep'? Well, it's wrong. True beauty goes so much deeper."

"Yes, it does. The Veil certainly proves that." Tara was delighted at seeing her sister so content. "And I've never seen you look more beautiful, Kandi."

"I know." Kandide beamed.

"Oh, well," Teren shrugged. His sister may have learned acceptance, but her vanity had certainly not diminished. "Did you also know that it was Mother who planted the original grapevines that grow here?"

"She did?" Kandide questioned.

"Yeah, with her own hands, too," Teren smiled. It was rare that he ever knew anything that Kandide didn't know. It was even rarer that she would admit it.

"Teren is right, my child," interjected Selena, who walked up to join them. "Your mother and I spent many a day getting those first cuttings started, and now just look at them." She gestured toward the vast field of grapes. With the weather still warm, they hadn't yet dropped their leaves. "I've been looking for you. It is almost time for dinner."

"Great!" Teren jumped up. "I'm starved!"

"Good. Shall we head back then?"

"Let's go!" Teren didn't wait for his sisters to answer.

As they began walking toward the château, Selena turned to Tara. "I think your father would have been so very proud of what we have accomplished. After we were settled and others began to arrive, the château was built, and then the gardens. The lake was rechanneled to allow for watering—and swimming."

She looked at Kandide and winked.

"It's really wonderful," Tara nodded. "Mother will be so happy to hear how very much you've accomplished. I know she misses you so much."

"I'm helping as well," Kandide interjected. "I'm making wings so Egan and Margay can fly."

"Wings? Fly?" Teren looked at Kandide, then back to Selena.

"Yes. I came up with a really great idea, and we were about to test it when Jake heard Ari's howl. Come, I'll show you."

"Hey, I want to go eat," Teren objected.

"You can eat later. Selena will hold dinner for us. Won't you, Selena?"

Selena looked at Tara, then at Teren, and shrugged, "Some things will never change. Don't be long."

"We won't." Kandide once again pulled the two of them away.

"But I'm hungry . . ."

"You can eat in a few minutes, Teren. Come on. Tomorrow we will have a feast to celebrate your arrival. Then we'll discuss what to do about Mother and the Council. I promise."

"Kandide," he moaned.

"Did you know that we have a hot spring?"

"Can it boil a potato?"

FORTY-NINE

W hat a feast the morrow brought. Jewel-encrusted goblets were filled and then refilled with beverages of every type. Tremendous silver platters contained honey-dipped sweet potatoes, wild rice topped with acorn-stuffed mushrooms, fresh creamed rhubarb in a banana-lime sauce, and all types of other delicacies. No sooner was one tray emptied than another replaced it. Bright green avocados were tossed with cranberries, grapes, apples, mangoes, and pineapple to make a colorful salad. And there were at least a dozen different fresh-baked breads, cakes, and pies, plus all types of cheeses and fruits, along with nuts and berries the likes of which Teren and Tara had never seen.

Baked pumpkin pudding topped with cinnamon, nutmeg, and cloves was served steaming hot, fresh from the oven. It smelled incredible and tasted even better. Teren went back three times for more. He also couldn't stop eating the elegantly decorated marzipan candies and the dark chocolate swirls that were filled with almonds and cherries.

Neither sibling had ever been to a feast with so much incredible food, gaiety, and splendor. Tara's crowning parties could not even begin to compare. Harpists and bards filled the room with music and wondrous stories—followed by dancing, juggling, acrobats, and magicians—then more delicious treats. Even Teren showed off a trick or two, much to the delight of the younger Fée. The feast lasted well into the wee hours of the morning. They had never danced, eaten, or laughed so much.

Tara was especially struck by the fact that all of this—all of the splendor and happiness—had been created by Fée who were discarded by their own, sent away as though they were just so much rubbish. And in spite of it all, there seemed to be no hatred or anger among any of them. Just a love of life and a true appreciation for all that it had to offer. It didn't matter if someone had two legs or none, was blind or missing an arm, all were respected as individuals—not for what they looked like, but for who they were and what they were able to contribute.

Stuffed from all of the food, and somewhat exhausted from all of the dancing, Tara plopped down on the thickly upholstered settee next to her brother to catch her breath.

"Chocolate?" he offered.

"Gosh, no. I don't think I'll ever eat again!"

"Okay." He popped the remaining piece left on his plate into his mouth. "Good thing our chefs don't know how to make these. I'd be as fat as Lady Batony!"

"Teren!" she reprimanded. "That's not nice."

"Okay, not that fat!"

"Lady Batony's not fat."

"She's not all that thin, either. But I like her, crazy as she is sometimes." He helped himself to a couple more pieces of chocolate from a tray that was being passed around.

"Why can't the rest of the world be like this?" Tara sighed, as she looked across the crowded hall at all the gaiety. She couldn't help but notice that Kandide seemed to not only accept, but also to truly respect her newfound friends.

"I don't know. But maybe if Kandide can change, there's hope for everyone else, too. Hey, I learned a new spell! Want to see it?"

"I do, but right now I'm more concerned with when we'll be able to get Kandi to return home. I don't know what will happen if the Frost isn't deployed by the Winter Solstice, but it's not going to be good. You saw those grapes; they should have been just bare vines by now." Tara shook her head as she looked over at her sister, who had been dancing all night— mostly with Jake.

Teren was also watching Kandide. "I think she's in love with him."

"I think you're right. Maybe Jake can convince her to come with us."

"Yeah, it's not like she can't come right back here after deploying it. Hey, we could ask Jake to come along."

"That's a thought."

"Or, maybe Kandide could just try deploying the Gift from here," Teren suggested. "It might work."

"You know it won't. It only works from the castle."

"I wonder why."

"I'm not exactly sure. But I do know that's why the castle was built on that particular spot. It has to do with the convergence of the three energy flows that intersect at that point."

"I have an idea. If Kandide won't leave by tomorrow, I'll put a spell on her and we'll take her back that way."

"Think it would work?" If all else failed, Tara certainly would not object.

"It's worth a try!"

FIFTY

The next morning, following a very late breakfast, Kandide and Tara left the dining room to join Jake, Teren, and Selena around the large bejeweled fireplace in the Great Hall. As they walked into the room, Tara was still pleading with her sister. "We must return soon, Kandi. You know time is running out."

"I'm afraid she's right, Kandide." As much as Jake didn't like the thought of Kandide leaving, he had to agree with Tara. "If you don't return soon, Tiyana will certainly feel obligated to use what little of the Gift she has. It probably will take all of her strength."

"It might even kill her!" Teren was desperate to persuade his sister to go back with them. "Mom's not all that young anymore, you know." Realizing that Selena and his mother were exactly the same age, he looked at his aunt rather sheepishly, quickly adding, "Oh, uh . . . Selena, I didn't mean it that way. She's not like . . . really old!"

Kandide ignored her brother. "The Council will just have to wait a little longer. I simply do not wish to go back right now."

"You are right, Kandide, you cannot go back," Selena calmly reassured her.

"Selena?" Tara was flabbergasted at her aunt's statement. "She must—"

Raising a hand to silence her young niece, Selena continued, "You can never go back, even if your wing is completely healed. However, you can go forward. The past is like a library, a wonderful place for learning, but not for living. What you must do now, Kandide, is to use what you have learned here at the Veil to teach others, so that they can also go forward and create a better world for all Fée."

From behind a chair, Egan peeked out. His newly formed wings were firmly strapped to his back. Climbing onto Kandide's lap, he remarked, "Kandide, my mother sent me away too. But if she could see me now, maybe she would change her mind." Egan's brand-new wings almost hit her in the face as he proudly fluttered them. "Even if she didn't, I wouldn't want her to die, just 'cause of me."

A deep frown crossed Kandide's face. Feeling the feather in her pocket, a thought suddenly occurred to her. With an excited smile, she spread Egan's wings apart so she could see the others. Knocking the young Fée off her lap, she abruptly stood up. "I have an idea! Oh, sorry, Egan, but you've given me a terrific idea."

FIFTY-ONE

"I did? I gave you an idea, Kandide?" Egan was beside himself at the thought.

Turning to Tara and her brother, Kandide politely ordered, "Prepare to leave."

"Then you'll go?" Teren exclaimed, jumping up. "You'll go now, Kandide?" He wasn't sure what had changed her mind, but he wasn't about to argue.

"You'll come back with us . . . right now?" Tara was also surprised.

"Yes," Kandide asserted. "Jake and Selena must also accompany us."

"That's great!" Thrilled at the prospect, Teren looked back and forth between the two of them.

"I'm afraid that I cannot," Selena responded. "I must remain here."

Diana S. Zimmerman

"Why, Selena?" Kandide quizzed.

"As much as I would love to see my sister again, I fear that if I am seen, it will raise far too many questions and the Veil might be discovered. Everything that we have worked so hard to achieve could be jeopardized. You'll be in good hands with Jake." Selena patted him on the shoulder.

"Then let's go!" With that, Teren gestured to transport, but nothing happened. He tried again, and still nothing happened. Neither he nor the others vanished. "I . . . I don't understand." He looked at Jake, then Kandide.

"It's the Veil," Jake explained.

"In order to protect us," Kandide added, "Father put an enchantment on this area so that no one can transport directly in or out."

"Is that why we arrived outside, in the Mists?" Tara looked from Jake to Selena.

"That is why," she answered, nodding her head. "It could be quite dangerous if just anyone could enter."

"It's pretty dangerous if they don't!" Teren quipped.

"Normally, the garglans don't come this close," Jake continued. "I've never seen so many of them. One or two, maybe, possibly even three, but never a dozen!"

"Thirteen," Teren corrected. "There were thirteen."

"Perhaps with the weather so warm," Selena suggested, "they are looking for water. In any case, you must leave the grounds, beyond the edge of the Veil, before transporting will work."

"Well, if you think Ari and his friends will protect us once more, then let's be going." Tara also stood up.

"Are you coming, Jake?" Kandide turned to head for the door.

"I guess I am," he nodded.

"I guess we all are!" Tara proclaimed.

"Be very careful, my children," Selena called after them.

Just as they entered the Mists, Kandide spotted Egan sneaking along behind. "Egan, what are you doing here?"

"I want to go, too," he replied, popping out from behind a large tangled bush.

"Not this time." Kandide was emphatic. "Maybe later. Now hurry back inside."

"I don't think he can." Jake pointed toward a nearby tree. "Look!" Two garglans, lurking in the branches above, snarled and hissed. "In fact, I think we all need to leave . . . right now!"

One of the garglans leapt from the tree. Instantly, Jake gestured and all five of them vanished. The garglans' only meal that day was a spray of faery dust.

A hush befell the High Council,
except for Lady Aron who gasped.

FIFTY-TWO

I nside the chamber of the High Council, the anxious members were all assembled, as they had been each day since Teren and Tara left.

"How could you have let Tara go with him, Tiyana?" drilled Lady Aron in her normal condescending manner.

"I've already told you, I did not let her go!" Tiyana was completely fed up with Lady Aron's nonstop badgering. "And just in case you have forgotten, Tara is our queen. I could hardly prohibit her from doing anything she wants to do."

"Have you at least heard from them?" There was an undertone of sarcasm in Lady Aron's voice.

"No, I have not," Tiyana snapped.

"Well, since you don't even know if any of your children are still alive, I really must insist that we proceed as though Kandide, and possibly even Queen Tara and Prince Teren, are not coming back." Lady Aron was almost smiling. She was more determined than ever to take charge of this situation. "We all know what will happen if the seasons do not change."

"Well, Lady Aron, for fear of disappointing you, we are all still alive." Kandide, along with the others, suddenly appeared inside the chamber.

A stunned hush befell the High Council, except for Lady Aron, who gasped.

"Kandide!" Tiyana rushed over to embrace her daughter. "Kandide, you are safe!"

Glancing around at the assembly, she answered, "Yes, Mother, I am." Giving Tiyana a warm embrace, she continued: "I'd like you to meet some very special friends of mine. This is Jake and . . . and . . . Egan." Looking around, she realized he was hiding behind her cape. "Well, the young lad behind me is Egan."

"Jake? It can't be!" An astonished Lady Socrat leapt to her feet and rushed over to him. "Is it you? Is it really you?"

"Yes, Mother, it's me."

"What?" Kandide looked at him.

"But how?" An equally astonished Lord Socrat hurried over to Jake as well. "We searched everywhere for you—for years. What happened? Where have you been all this time?"

Throwing their arms around him, Lady Socrat began to cry tears of joy. "I can't believe it! My son! I can't believe it."

Kandide stared at Jake in amazement. "Your mother and father? You never told me."

Looking at Kandide, Jake smiled, hugging his parents. "It wasn't important until now."

None, however, was more surprised than Lady Aron. "Kandide ... Prince Teren ... how did you . . . ? Uh ... I mean ... it's good to see that you are safe. You as well, Tara." Quickly regaining her composure, she continued, "And you, Jake, it's been a while—a long while. However, we have more important things to discuss right now than family reunions. Kandide, you must relinquish the Gift of the Frost, and you must do it immediately!"

"Nice to see you as well, Lady Aron," Jake sarcastically retorted.

"Well?" Lady Aron insisted, ignoring him and staring straight at Kandide.

"I have returned, and as you can see, the Gift is strong." Her radiance was glowing even more than normal. "And yes, I will, of course, be happy to transfer it."

"Good!" Lady Aron replied, more than a little surprised. "Then do it, immediat—"

"There is, however, a price," Kandide cut her off.

"A price?" Lady Aron fired back. "How dare you!"

"No, how dare you, Lady Aron," Kandide challenged.

"There will be no bargaining!"

"Fine, then I shall be off." Kandide started to gesture.

Lord Aron's attention had been momentarily diverted as he stared at Egan. He quickly turned back to the conversation. "Wait! I say wait! What is this price you seek, Kandide?" Lady Aron started to protest, but he quickly silenced her. "Please, my dear, let us at least hear Kandide out."

Standing very tall and looking incredibly regal, Kandide declared, "For the Gift of the Frost, I humbly demand a change in the Articles to allow all Imperfects the full rights and privileges of the Fée."

"That is preposterous!" Lady Aron was seething with anger. "Never will we allow the superiority of our clans to be compromised by permitting Imperfects to live among us! They will have no rights, and they certainly will never be our equals."

"I only ask that they be treated equally." Kandide was far more stately in her tone. "Equality, like respect, my dear Lady Aron, must be earned. Even humankind has proclaimed that 'all men are created equal,' not that they all 'become equal.' It is individual validity that I seek, so that each may have the full rights and privileges to determine his or her destiny. I do hope that clarifies my demand."

"You tell her, Kandide!" Teren exclaimed. In all his life, he would have never believed his sister possible of speaking such words. And at that moment, he couldn't have been more proud.

The members of the High Council, however, were not nearly so impressed. They began to murmur among themselves, their conversations becoming more and more at odds with one another.

Once again, it was Lady Aron who spoke out. "Your demand will never be met, not as long as I have a vote."

Kandide surveyed the group, focusing directly upon the fiery Fée. "Fine," she replied almost too calmly. Turning to Jake and then to Tiyana, she continued, "I am sorry, Mother, I have made my offer. Since it seems as though the Council will not even consider it, I see no reason to remain here any longer. Shall we be off, Jake?"

FIFTY-THREE

"You can't leave, Kandi," Tara insisted. "As queen, I . . . I . . . well, I forbid it!"

"Bravo, Tara!" Teren was thrilled by his sister taking control. "I mean . . . Your Majesty."

"Let her go, Tara," Tiyana implored. She was appalled and disgusted at seeing the Council in such disarray. "Kandide is right to want to leave. Since the uniting of the clans, we have advanced in so many ways, yet we are still so very barbaric in others. I just do not understand why. Many of you have lost loved ones because of these arcane laws, and yet you continue to uphold them. Will we never gain a social conscience?"

Once again, the Council members broke out in a flurry of comments, each speaking over the other.

"Stop! All of you!" insisted Lord Rössi, in an attempt to quiet the ruckus. "Please, Kandide, give us a few minutes. I suggest that the Council discuss this in proper fashion. Jake has survived all this time, and his injuries seem to have fully healed. Perhaps there are healing treatments that we do not know about."

"I would say that I have overcome my injuries, but not that they've been cured." Clearly illustrating that he still had no feet, Jake flew up into the air, leaving his boots on the floor.

Gasps rang out from the Council members. "This is outrageous!" Lady Aron exclaimed. Having nearly fainted from the shock, she hurriedly fanned herself. "I will have none of this mockery!"

"Neither shall I, Lady Aron." Kandide turned and started walking toward the chamber door.

"Wait! Please . . . all of you." Once again, all eyes turned toward Tara. "As your queen, I command the Council to discuss this rationally. And . . . and that you, Kandi, give me this day so that I may make your case before the High Council. Please?"

"Well stated, Your Majesty," chimed in Lord Rössi. "The Council accepts your order. Kandide, would you, Jake, Teren, and your young friend please consider waiting in the ante-chamber while Tara and I try to make some sense out of all this with the Council?"

"As you please, my lord." Kandide graciously bowed, but only with her head, and with a very stiff posture. Then, looking straight at Lady Aron, she unflinchingly declared, "I shall give you one hour."

"That is hardly enough time," Lady Aron retorted, her amber eyes blazing.

"Take it or not," came Kandide's mocking response.

She, Jake, Teren, and Egan, who continued to hide behind Kandide's cloak, turned and left the Council chamber.

"How come you look like me?"

FIFTY-FOUR

"Mother! Mother!" A young faery boy called excitedly as he flew into the Council's antechamber where Kandide, Egan, Teren, and Jake were waiting. "Oh!" He landed rather abruptly. "Are you Princess Kandide?"

She turned and looked at him rather quizzically. "Yes. And who . . . who are you?"

"I'm Alin, son of Lord and Lady Aron," he answered with a most gracious and sweeping bow.

While Kandide knew they had a son, she hadn't seen him since he was a baby. "You're Lord and Lady Aron's son?"

"I am!"

Egan was standing behind Kandide. He peeked out from one side of her cape. To his surprise, he saw his twin, a young faery who looked exactly like him. He quickly leaned to the other side, as if to hide. Noticing him, Alin did the same, mimicking his actions from side to side, trying to get a better glimpse.

Finally, Alin broke their game of back and forth. "How come you look like me?" he asked with a curious frown.

"How come you look like me?" Egan responded, also frowning.

"I don't know," answered Alin.

"Are we twins?" Egan asked, sizing him up and down.

"Maybe," Alin shrugged as they looked at each other again. "Why are your wings funny?"

"Because they are prototypes," Egan proclaimed, proudly showing them off.

"Wow!" Not at all sure what Egan meant by "prototypes," Alin quickly added, "Can you fly with them?"

"Of course I can!" Egan responded just as quickly.

"So, let me see." Alin motioned for him to do so.

"Okay!" Egan attempted to fly. Unfortunately, with no wind to help him lift off, he couldn't quite do it.

Noticing that he was having trouble, Teren gestured to create an air current, and Egan sailed right up, gleefully flying around the room. "See . . . see. I told you so!" he proudly squealed.

"Wow, they're really nice." Alin flew up to him. Giggling, the two of them played a quick game of tag as they flitted back and forth.

"I can do something else, too," Egan added, landing rather unsteadily. Landing was something he was still getting used to.

"What?"

"I can swim!"

"No you can't!" Shaking his head, Alin did not quite believe him.

"Can too!" Egan insisted. "Can't I, Kandide?"

"Yes, you can," she responded. "You are my best student."

"Wow!" Alin exclaimed. "Do you think you could teach me how to swim? My mom won't go near the water. She's from the Fire clan and my dad is Earthen, so he won't even try."

"Sure!" Egan responded. "Can I, Kandide? Can I?"

"I don't see why not." The two of them started to run off. "Not right now, however," she called after them.

"Okay," Egan answered. "Maybe we can go later. Want to see how my wings work?"

"Sure," Alin replied.

The two of them raced over to a large chair.

"Stay near, where I can see you." Kandide's words fell on deaf ears. The two children were lost in the fun of getting to know each other and exploring Egan's "prototypes." "We may be leaving soon," she called after them.

"With all due respect, Queen Tara, you know that cannot possibly be true. Do you not realize that the sanctity of the Fée is at risk?"

FIFTY-FIVE

Inside the Council Chamber, the discussion was getting hotter and hotter.

"Respectfully, Your Majesty, I must insist that you tell the Council where you found Kandide." Lady Aron was almost shouting as she attempted to get Tara to reveal the secret of the Mists for all to hear.

"I've already told you," Tara responded in a quieter than normal voice, "Teren and I simply ran into the three of them in the woods. That is all I can tell you."

"With all due respect, Queen Tara, you know that cannot possibly be true. Do you not realize that the sanctity of the Fée is at risk?" It was all Lady Aron could do to remember that Tara was, indeed, their queen.

"I do not believe that to be the case, Lady Aron," interjected Lord Socrat.

"Nor do I," Lady Karena agreed.

"Nor I," Lady Batony spoke up. "Why, when I was a young gir—"

"When you were a young girl, Lady Batony, the individual clans controlled such matters." Lady Aron was livid. "Perhaps it should be that way again!"

"Ladies, please! Can you try to stay on track—just this once?" Lord Rössi glared at the two of them.

"For some of us, that seems to be quite difficult," Lady Aron replied.

"And for others, downright impossible," Lady Batony retorted. "I do, however, think you should at least try, Firenza."

"I have an idea, why don't you both try?" Lord Rössi was quickly losing patience with these two. "Now, as the Council Chair, if there is no more discussion, I call for the vote. As protocol dictates, each member can vote only once, using only the acorns placed in front of him or her. White is for yes; black is for no; green is to abstain. Only a unanimous vote may amend the Articles and all abstentions will go to the prevailing side."

"The matter on the floor," he continued, "is to amend the Articles to allow Imperfects full rights and privileges of the Fée. As Chair, I must place the first vote. While I do not believe that all Fée are ready to accept Imperfects, I do believe that history has shown the alternatives to be far worse. Therefore, the acorn I place in the center is white."

"Lord Socrat, how do ye vote?" he continued.

"'Tis a policy that cost me a son. Now I may have him back. I vote Yea." He proudly pushed his white acorn forward.

"Lady Socrat, how do ye vote?"

"I, too, vote Yea. May no other parent ever suffer such a loss." She pushed her white acorn forward.

"My fair, Lady Corale?"

Shoving the white acorn toward the center, she stated, "I follow their lead. It is time we look to the future."

"Lady Alicia?"

"My clan has desired to accept Imperfects almost since the Treaty was signed. I vote Yea." She moved her white acorn forward.

"Lord Salitar?" he continued.

"There is no real choice. Kandide's terms are most persuasive. My vote is Yea." He pushed his white acorn to the center as well.

"Lord Standish?"

"I feel that my decision will not be well received by many members of my clan. I am, however, designated to do what I think is best. Certainly, the argument for the Frost must prevail. Therefore, I accept the amendment." He placed his white acorn in the center with the rest.

"Lord Revên?"

"I may well be removed from the Council by my own clan's High Court for my decision. However, as Lord Standish just stated, the Frost must be given precedence or all life shall suffer." He also shoved his white acorn to the center.

"Lady Karena?"

"Perhaps now all Fée can learn to accept Imperfects, and perhaps in doing so, we will all grow stronger. My acorn is, without question, white."

"Lady Batony?"

"As most of you know, it is rare that I ever side with the majority—although not rare that I disagree with Lady Aron. In this case, I must agree that Kandide, as is more often than not the case, has left us with no other choice. The Gift, and therefore the Frost, must take precedence. White it is." She responded by adding her white acorn to the pile.

"Lord Aron, how do ye vote?"

Gazing at his wife, he hesitated only briefly, and then placed his white acorn in the center of the table. "The time for acceptance is long overdue."

"Lady Aron, how do ye vote?"

Glaring at her husband with both shock and anger, she picked up the black acorn and started to push it forward. Before she could do so, however, Lord Aron grabbed her wrist to stop her.

"Hear me, first," he stated, and then turned to the Council. "Not so many years ago, Lady Aron and I bore two sons. Twins they were, identical in every way but one. My Lady could not bear the shame of a son who was born without wings, so I was given the task of sending our newly born child away. Instead, I brought him to King Toeyad in hopes that his healers could help. It was the last I saw of him until today."

"You did what?" a stunned Lady Aron shrieked.

"What do you mean, today?" Tiyana asked.

"May the earthly spirits help us, but I am fairly certain that the lad with Kandide is our other son," Lord Aron responded.

"That is a lie!" Lady Aron protested. "How dare you tell this tale! Our second son passed at birth, and he . . . he was perfect!" She was holding onto the black acorn so tightly it literally combusted in her hand, leaving nothing but ash.

Realizing what had just happened, Lord Rössi was determined to take advantage of the moment. "How do ye vote, Lady Aron?"

Looking at what was, just moments before, a black acorn, Lady Aron realized that she could no longer vote Nay. "This is unfair," she declared. "I demand another black acorn!"

"You know the rules. Each member must vote using only the acorns given. How do ye vote, Lady Aron?" Lord Rössi was most insistent.

Having no choice, she angrily pushed the green acorn forward. Glaring at her husband, she cried, "You'll regret this day!" Turning toward the other Council members, she screeched, "You will all regret what is done here!"

Ignoring her words, Lord Rössi calmly proclaimed, "Since Lady Aron abstains, her vote goes with the majority. The Articles shall be amended. Let it be known that from this day forward, Imperfects have full rights and privileges."

Amid sighs of relief from the Council, Lady Aron repeated her warning, "Mark my words, you will all live to regret this decision!" She stormed out of the chamber.

"You'll pay for this!
You will all pay for this."

FIFTY-SIX

"Mother ... Mother, look! I have a twin!" Alin shouted, spotting his mother as she entered the antechamber.

Walking over to him, Lady Aron grabbed her son's arm. "What are you talking about?"

Excited, Alin replied, "Mother, this is Egan. Look, he's my twin! Father said I had a brother who was lost when we were born. I've found him!"

"You have no brother!" she declared. "And if you did, he certainly would not be an Imperfect!" Glowering at Egan in sheer disgust, she started to pull Alin away.

"But ... but Mother, he looks just like me—and he's going to teach me how to swim."

"It is merely a cruel trick of glamour. Your brother passed when he was born!"

"No! No . . . he's here!" Alin pleaded. "I know it!"

Lady Aron stared directly at a frightened Egan, and, as if willing him to be so, she coldly reiterated, "Your brother is dead!"

"But he's not . . ." Alin was in tears as she dragged him away.

Turning to Kandide, Lady Aron screeched, "You'll pay for this! You will all pay for this!" With a wave of her hand, she and a sobbing Alin disappeared.

"Egan . . ." Alin called as his voice trailed off.

Tears began streaming down Egan's face. He looked up at Kandide. "Am I his brother? Is she my mother?"

FIFTY-SEVEN

"You've done it, Kandi! Oh, Kandi! You've done it!" Tara raced out of the Council chamber.

Kandide was astonished. "You mean . . . ?"

"Yes! The Articles are to be amended!" Tara exclaimed.

"Yes! Yes! Yes!" Teren hollered, jumping up and down while hoisting his fist in the air three times to match his words.

"There is one stipulation, however," interjected Lord Rössi, who, along with the other Council members, followed Tara out of the chamber.

"Stipulation, Lord Rössi?" Kandide looked at him askance.

"Now that Imperfects are to have full rights, you must agree to return as queen."

"Oh, Kandi, please say yes." Tara rushed over to her. "Please!"

Diana S. Zimmerman

"I . . . I . . ." Stymied, Kandide looked at Tara, then Jake, and at the rest of the Council.

Lord Socrat smiled, quickly adding, "Tara has abdicated the throne to pursue her other duties. Which means that you can assume your rightful place as our queen, Kandide."

Kandide looked back at Tara, then to Jake, and finally over to Lord Socrat. Shaking her head, she answered, "No. I am afraid that I cannot be your Queen Kandide."

"Kandi, you must!" Tara thrust her crown at her sister. "This thing doesn't even fit my head."

"I will not be Queen Kandide. You may, however, call me Queen Kandi, the Crumplewing!" She winked at Jake, who beamed with pride. "Queen of *all* Fée!" she proudly insisted.

"That's perfect!" Tara shrieked, throwing her arms around her sister. "I mean, as you wish, Your Majesty." She ceremoniously placed the crown on Kandide's head, and then bowed, as did the rest of the High Council. Kandide humbly reciprocated.

"I went and got her!" Teren smugly remarked, ever so proud of both of his sisters—and himself, of course.

Kandide smiled at her brother. "You did, indeed, little brother, and risked your life to do so. How many garglans did you kill?"

"Thirteen, but who's counting—and Tara helped."

Amid the myriad of congratulatory comments, Kandide spotted Egan. Sitting all alone in a corner, his big blue eyes were full of tears. Seeing her look at him, he quickly stood up. Attempting a smile, he bowed with a very well-mannered "Congratulations, Your Majesty."

"Egan, come here with me." Kandide reached out to take his hand.

Seeing the two of them together, Lord Aron hastily walked over, politely requesting, "Your Majesty, would you do me the honor of introducing this young lad to me? I think it is time we get to know each other."

Hardly able to contain her delight, Kandide responded, "Of course. Egan, this is Lord Aron—your father."

Confused, Egan frowned, skeptically looking up at him. "You . . . you . . . are my father?"

"Yes, I am—that is, if you will have me."

Cautiously, the young Fée asked, "Aren't you ashamed of me, too?"

With tears welling up in his eyes, Lord Aron knelt in front of his son and held out his hands. "It is you who should be ashamed of me. Will you accept me as your father?"

Egan jumped into his arms, hugging him so tightly that he almost knocked both of them over. "Kandide, I have a father!"

"You certainly do, and a very nice one at that."

"I really have a father!"

"And I have my other son back. Thank you, Your Majesty."

Walking over to the large window, Kandide opened it. She began breathing in and out, in and out—very slowly and very deeply. Finally, after several minutes, she gestured into the air with both hands. Energy surged through her body. As the essence of the Gift flowed from her fingertips, a streak of lightning high in the atmosphere lit up the entire sky. A split second later, a booming clap of thunder was heard. The outside temperature suddenly dropped and the leaves on the trees began to sparkle.

"Look!" Egan cried. Jumping out of his father's arms, he pushed his way through the Council members to look out the window. "The Frost, it's starting! Father, look!"

All the land began to shimmer with a delicate blanket of icy crystals as the season's first Frost started to form.

Looking very pale and feeling extremely faint from having used virtually all of her strength to deploy the Gift, Kandide managed to make it to the nearest chair. Her breathing was heavy and she was completely drained. The radiance that normally surrounded her was now only a subtle glow.

Jake rushed over to her. Kneeling down, he gently squeezed her hand. "I'm so very proud of you, Kandide. I mean, Your Majesty." Bowing, he looked into her eyes. "So very proud."

"Call me Kandi," she whispered with an impish smile. "And for goodness sake, please stop bowing."

Filled with excitement, Jake kissed her hand, then went over to his parents, and with more hugs, began filling them in on his life in the Mists.

Still looking outside, Egan spotted Alin and timidly waved. Looking up at Lord Aron, he asked, "Do . . . do you think Mother will ever like me?"

Lifting his son up, Lord Aron gazed into the courtyard, quietly answering, "Some Fée are just going to need more time."

"Sure she will," Teren piped in, not wanting anything to spoil the magic of this incredible moment.

Lord Aron forced a not-all-too-sure smile at Teren, and then hugged his son. "Sure she will. Give her time."

"Hey, Tara, now do you want to see my new spell?"

Teren asked.

"I'd love to." Thrilled to be relieved of her courtly duties, Tara took off with her brother. They were both eager to be finished with politics of any kind.

Seeing Kandide alone, Tiyana walked over and knelt beside her daughter. "Queen for only a few moments and look at what you have already accomplished. Your father would be so very happy and proud."

"It was a stunning plan, wasn't it?"

"Yes, it was. I'm proud of you as well, Kandide."

"Thank you, Mother. Hearing you say that means a lot to me."

Tiyana hugged her daughter. "Very proud of you." Seeing Kandide looking at Jake, she smiled. "Why don't you ask him?"

"Ask him what?"

"To rule by your side, of course," Tiyana gently responded.

A bit surprised by her mother's comment, Kandide stammered, "I . . . I . . ."

"He is crazy about you."

"Well, of course he is, but shouldn't he ask me?" Taking her mother's arm to help steady herself, Kandide stood up. She was still weak and shaky from deploying the Gift.

"Protocol, my daughter. You must ask him. After all, you are queen."

Outside, snowflakes were beginning to fall and everything sparkled with a crystal-like glow. Winter was finally on its way and the courtyard was full of younglings who were flittering about laughing and joking while throwing snowballs as fast as they could make them. Everyone seemed to be enjoying the change in the seasons. It may have been a late winter, but it certainly had all the makings of a great one. Perhaps, with the amending of the Articles, it was also the time for *all* life to begin anew.

With Tiyana's help, Kandide walked to the balcony and looked out. It was, indeed, a beautiful site. Contemplating her mother's words, she looked at Tiyana, then to Jake, and back toward the snow-covered courtyard. A pleased smile crossed her face. "A winter wedding . . . I do look extraordinary in white!"

Suddenly, Tara and Teren came rushing back into the room.

"Kandide! I mean, Queen Kandi," Teren exclaimed, "There's trouble."

"What . . . what is it?" Kandide turned to look at her brother and sister.

"It's the Banshees," Tara chimed in. "Thousands of their troops are amassing along the neutral zone."

"Oh, dear," Tiyana exclaimed. "Your father feared King Nastae might try something. That is one of the reasons why he wanted your crowning to take place so quickly, Kandide."

Looking from her mother to Tara and then over to Teren, Kandide was still very pale. Unsure what else to do, she replied, "Gather my generals. We meet in an hour."

With a gesture, she was gone.

"Why, Princess Tara? Why?
All who love you will have a very long
winter to ponder that question."

PREVIEW OF BOOK TWO: THE LADY'S REVENGE

"Well, Tara," Lady Aron sighed, "I guess it is finally time to implement part two of my plan. I do apologize for being slightly behind schedule, but then, one must be flexible in these matters, you know. You must also believe me when I say that I am truly sorry, my dear. You, I almost like."

Tara had no idea what Lady Aron was up to, but she knew it was not going to be good. She also knew that these might be the last words she ever spoke. "You'll never get away with this . . . Firenza. My sister will destroy you."

"Yes, so you told me." Lady Aron simply smiled at her. "I am, however, most grateful that you are so very concerned for my welfare."

"Why are you doing this? At least tell me that."

"Why, Princess Tara? Why? All who love you will have a very long winter to ponder that question."

Turning to the guards, Lady Aron ordered, "Now, I need each of you to start breathing in time with me. It will take all of our combined energies to make this work."

She began rhythmically inhaling and exhaling. As the guards joined hands with her to form a circle, each of them matched her breathing pattern. Within seconds, sparks began to fly and the mounting energy from their bodies transferred into Lady Aron.

"More," she demanded. "Breathe faster! Faster!"

Helpless to do anything, Tara struggled to get free. She could not even imagine what was about to happen.

Suddenly, all of their combined energies converged directly into the fiery Fée. "Keep breathing!" she screeched. With a few mumbled words, Lady Aron made an abrupt gesture toward the terrified Princess. Within seconds, her plan for Tara was, indeed, put into place. "You can stop now," she casually instructed.

Exuberant, Lady Aron stepped back to admire her work. "Perfect, if I do say so myself. It's time for you to return home, my dear, sweet Tara." She gestured again, "Off you go," and Tara was gone.

Turning to her captain, Lady Aron casually smiled. "I guess it's also time for the unfortunate, but highly necessary, part of my plan." She made yet another sweeping gesture, and instantly the three guards were literally incinerated in bright sequential flashes. Only the silhouettes of their bodies remained, forever etched on the walls of the Banshee cave.

"Pity I can't do that with Fée that are not of the Fire clan."

Lady Aron again smiled at the captain. "It would make my life so much easier." There was absolutely no semblance of remorse in her voice.

"Was . . . was that really necessary?" he stammered. "They were some of your most loyal soldiers."

"Now, Captain, you know I cannot have any witnesses . . . not even one!"

Glaring at her, the captain barely had a chance to react before he was also incinerated.

"I'm not sure which I will find more amusing," she chortled. "The look on my fine captain's face—he was such a loyal soldier—or that of Kandide's when she reads this note."

Lady Aron placed a rolled-up parchment on Tara's empty blanket. "Now it is time for me to be off. The next part of my plan should be even more amusing."

ABOUT THE CHARACTERS

KANDIDE

Age: 19 (in human years)
Height: 5'5"
Eyes: Purple-blue
Hair: Gold and platinum
Hobbies: Archery, aercaen, swimming, preening
Heroes: King Toeyad, and myself, of course
Favorite
  Book: Book One: *Kandide and the Secret of the Mists*,
            Book Two: *Kandide and the Lady's Revenge*,
            Book Three: *Kandide and the Flame is Fleeting*
            (Because they're about me!)
Quote: "Equality, like respect, my dear Lady Aron, must
            be earned."

PRINCE TEREN

Age: 14 (in human years)
Height: 5'
Eyes: Yellow-brown
Hair: Sandy blond
Hobbies: Spell-making, pranks, wizardry, aercaen
Heroes: Merlin, Viviana, and most other wizards
Favorite
   Book: Book Three: *Kandide and the Flame is Fleeting*
            (Because I get to be a hero.)
Quote: "Gosh, Kandide's vain!"

PRINCESS TARA

Age:	16 (in human years)
Height:	5'4"
Eyes:	Green
Hair:	Auburn
Hobbies:	Healing, saving forest animals, and keeping her sister and brother out of trouble
Heroes:	Selena, Queen Tiyana
Favorite Book:	Book Three: *Kandide and the Flame is Fleeting* (I can't tell you; it would spoil the ending.)
Quote:	"Why can't the rest of the world be like this?"

LADY ARON

Age: None of your business!
Height: 5'6"
Eyes: Amber and blue
Hair: Flaming
Hobbies: Archery, politics, and wizardry
            (Is there anything else?)
Heroes: Me. Who else?
Favorite
  Book: Book Two: *Kandide and the Lady's Revenge*
            (Isn't it obvious?)
Quote: "You will all regret what is done here!"

JAKE

Age:	27 (in human years)
Height:	5'11"
Eyes:	Green
Hair:	Black
Hobbies:	Archery, swimming, reading, dancing
Heroes:	King Toeyad, Selena, Trump, Ari
Favorite Book:	Book Three: *Kandide and the Flame is Fleeting* (It's really an adventure.)
Quote:	"I don't think I repulse you. I think you repulse you!"

LEANNE

Age:	21 (in human years)
Height:	5'3"
Eyes:	Brown
Hair:	Dark brown
Hobbies:	Healing, dancing, singing
Heroes:	Selena, Jake, Trust, and Ari
Favorite Book:	Book One: *Kandide and the Secret of the Mists* (Kandide comes into our lives.)
Quote:	"It's okay. I heal with my hands, not my eyes."

GARGLAN

Age: 37 (in human years)
Height: 5'
Eyes: Red
Hair: Brown and black patches
Hobbies: Eating Fée
Heroes: Me
Favorite
  Book: Book Four (maybe we win in that one)
Quote: "Grrrr . . . Hisssss!"

PLACES AND PEOPLE
IN BOOKS ONE, TWO, AND THREE

Adriana	Viviana and Centrod's daughter
Aercaen	Aerial cane-fighting game
Alin	Lord and Lady Aron's son
Anile	Banshee assassin
Aracno-beast	Huge spider/crablike creature
Ari	Wolf in the Mists
Asâe	Clan of the Ice and Snow
Bardic Council	Secret place of wizards
Benji	Imperfect/Jake's friend
Brandiar	Banshee
Calabiyau	Land of the Fée
Caluma	Banshee
Captain Asgart	Lady Aron's aide
Captain Bent	Banshee Redcap soldier
Captain Denan	Head of the Royal Guard
Captain Erley	Tara's guard
Captain Paulo	Guard
Captain Slant	Cyndara's number one guard
Centrod	Bardic High Priest
Chessaé	Four-tiered ancient chess game
Cotell	Signal to start aercaen
Courage	Gertie's griffin cub
Cushla	Banshee drink
Dura	Lady Aron's lady-in-waiting
Egan	Imperfect from the Veil/twin of Alin
Endor	Homing pigeon
Foggáe	Algae-fog that kills Fée
François de la Rochefoucauld	Human poet

Garglan	Goblin/gargoyle beast
General Kandour	Banshees' number one general
General Mintz	Kandide's number two general
General Pell	Kandide's number one general
Gertie	Mother griffin
Hectare	An area equal to 2.471 acres
Ilene	Imperfect from the Veil
Imperfect	Fée that isn't physically perfect
Jake	Kandide's love
Jessita	Imperfect from the Veil
Jola	Asgart's youngest child
King Nastae	Banshee king
King Toeyad	Calabiyau's king/Kandide's father
Lady Alicia	High Council member
Lady Batony	High Council member
Lady Corale	High Council member
Lady Firenza Aron	High Council member
Lady Karena	High Council member
Lady Maxella	"Grandmam," Alin's grandmother
Lady Socrat	High Council member
Leanne	Blind healer from the Veil
Lieutenant Frandal	Calabiyau guard
Lieutenant Kensel	Cyndara's messenger
Lieutenant Hobart	Calabiyau guard
Lieutenant Keightly	Royal guard
Lieutenant Minsee	Calabiyau guard
Lieutenant Randolf	Banshee traitor
Lieutenant Terrydale	Guard
Lindra	Imperfect from the Veil
Linal	Fire Fée from Calabiyau
Lord Aron	High Council member

Lord Mywerk	Half-wizard, half-Banshee
Lord Revên	High Council member
Lord Rössi	High Council member
Lord Salitar	High Council member
Lord Socrat	High Council member
Lord Standish	High Council member
Margay	Head cook in the Veil
Margrite	Imperfect from the Veil
Matari	500-year old in the Veil
Max Melini	Mywerk's grandfather, Merlin's grandson
Meter	Thirty-nine inches
Mylea	Kandide's number one lady-in-waiting
Palara	Captain Asgart's wife
Petre	Fire Fée from Calabiyau
Pixies	Fée who act as chessaé pieces
Prince Kilmonth	Cyndara's Banshee half-brother
Prince Teren	Kandide's brother
Prince Yandell	Cyndara's Banshee half-brother
Queen Cyndara	Ruler of the Banshees
Queen Kandide	Ruler of Calabiyau
Queen Tiyana	Kandide's mother
Salara	Imperfect from the Veil
Selena	Tiyana's twin sister
Sidue	Clan of the Forests
Socair	Soccerlike game played in the air
Tori	Imperfect/Jake's friend in the Veil
Trump	Imperfect Banshee
Trust	Wolf that saved Leanne
Tygad	Fire Fée from Calabiyau
Viviana	Bardic High Priestess

ABOUT THE AUTHOR

Like her novels, Diana's role in the performing arts as well as the business world transcends the ordinary. She has been a performer and businesswoman since the age of eight, when she invested all of her resources into a small magic trick. With a total capital outlay of forty-seven cents, Diana parlayed her investment into a spectacular twenty-five-year career as "America's Foremost Lady Magician." She has invented magic illusions for David Copperfield and Lance Burton, and is a highly respected lecturer, writer, and teacher in the world of magic. She also sponsors a young magicians' group—an organization she founded in 1974 with the help of Cary Grant at Hollywood's famous Magic Castle. Her transition to the corporate world saw the creation of CMS Communications, Intl., an international marketing communications agency whose clients include many of the Fortune 500. Diana is CMS's president and CEO. She is also an avid collector of faery art. With pieces dating back to the 1700s, her collection is one of the largest in the world. A painting by Australian artist Maxine Gadd, now in Diana's private collection, inspired the literary legacy of Kandide.

About the Illustrator

From the age of three, it was obvious that Maxine was an ex-traordinary talent. Born Maxine Saunders in Worcestershire, England, she was a shy child who preferred drawing to playing with friends. In 1967, her family immigrated to Australia. It was there that her artistic talents flourished. Maxine first exhib-ited her drawings at school and then at community art shows. She won numerous awards, and by the age of twelve was selling her paintings.

Always the nonconformist, at fifteen she chose to leave school, deciding instead to explore graphic design at a technical college. This, however, quickly became too restricting, and she left to focus on her own private world of art. But ever restless, Maxine longed to be involved with fellow artists. Even though college had been restrictive in the past, she decided to go back. After three years, she received a diploma in Graphic Design and won the prestigious John Lunghi Award for "Outstanding Artistic Design." Although Maxine paints many subjects, her distinctive approach to Fairies and Mermaids are what have truly captivated her fans.

www.fataraworld.com

COMING SOON FROM
DIANA S. ZIMMERMAN

KANDIDE AND THE LADY'S REVENGE

Book Two of the Calabiyau Chronicles

KANDIDE AND THE FLAME IS FLEETING

Book Three of the Calabiyau Chronicles

CONTINUE THE EXPERIENCE

Visit the official Kandide website: www.kandide.com
Play games such as the *Attack of the Garglans;* buy cool stuff;
check for author appearances; join Kandide's fan club; and get a
free newsletter. There are also links to other fantasy sites and
information about FaerieWorlds™ and FaerieCon,™ two amazing
weekends of faeries, fun, and fantasy. You can also preview and
pre-order Book Two: *Kandide and the Lady's Revenge* and Book Three:
Kandide and the Flame is Fleeting.

www.kandide.com